GR-

THE HOSTILE PEAKS

THE HOSTILE PEAKS

Louis Trimble

CHIVERS
THORNDIKE

This Large Print edition is published by BBC Audiobooks Ltd, Bath, England and by Thorndike Press®, Waterville, Maine, USA.

Published in 2004 in the U.K. by arrangement with Golden West Literary Agency.

Published in 2004 in the U.S. by arrangement with Golden West Literary Agency.

U.K. Hardcover ISBN 0–7540–9988–1 (Chivers Large Print)
U.K. Softcover ISBN 0–7540–9989–X (Camden Large Print)
U.S. Softcover ISBN 0–7862–6307–5 (Nightingale)

The text of this Large Print edition is unabridged.
Other aspects of the book may vary from the original edition.

Set in 16 pt. New Times Roman.

Printed in Great Britain on acid-free paper.

British Library Cataloguing in Publication Data available

Library of Congress Control Number: 2003116426

CHAPTER ONE

Clint Larabee stopped his chestnut at the top of a low summit and stared at the desolation stretching in front of him. As his eyes took in the chopped and gouged land that reached south and west to fold into the base of the towering Bitterroots, he began to understand for the first time how the army supply train had been so easily and thoroughly ambushed here.

Behind him lay the rich grasslands of the Big Hole Basin. And farther behind, the gold country—Bannack and Virginia, and the proud new capital of Montana Territory, Helena. Ahead, the land lay empty, with only small animals and an occasional bird stirring under the strangely warm October sun. It was hard for Larabee to believe that more fine grassland and the growing settlement of Glory Hole were less than a half hour's steady ride along this trail.

He squinted into the settling sun at the jagged peaks of the mountains, the higher ones already showing their caps of snow. Then he lowered his head and studied the well-ridden trail. At the foot of this low pass he could see where it branched—an obviously fresh piece laid out to follow what level ground there was in a big arc, and an equally obvious older one dipping quickly down into the dark depths of a high-walled canyon.

It was the old trail that interested Larabee and now he pushed the chestnut to the fork and down to the bottom of the narrow canyon. There was no sunshine here, but the afternoon light was strong enough to let him see as clearly as he needed.

A small stream came in abruptly from a side gully, meandered alongside the trail for a few hundred yards and then disappeared into a deep slash in the canyon's rocky south wall. Larabee paused to let the chestnut sample the icy water, and then he moved on, his eyes searching for the key spots marked on the map he carried.

Larabee nodded to himself. There was the spot, just past the narrow mouth of a gulch coming in from his right and this side of the mouth of a second gulch a hundred yards beyond on his left. When he passed the first gulch, he was able to see what few remains were left of that short, deadly fight—the picked-clean bones of a dead horse, empty shells, a shattered rifle stock, a bullet-gouged canteen.

Larabee swore bleakly. Four men had died in that fight. Four cavalry soldiers disguised as mule skinners, but armed and alerted to danger. Yet they had obviously been surprised, shot out of their saddles with no warning. Four dead and a fifth knocked from his horse and left to die on the rocky canyon floor.

'I can see how they got away easy enough,' he told the chestnut. 'In this maze, there'll be canyons to take a man almost anywhere he has a mind to go.'

The chestnut nickered as it always did when Larabee worked out his thinking aloud. Larabee grunted. 'The question isn't how the raiders got away with thirty mules loaded with ammunition, but what they did with it.'

The chestnut nickered again. *What and where?* Those were Larabee's questions. And even being here brought him no closer to an answer than he had been when he left Fort Hall those long weeks back. He had found no signs in Helena, in Bannack, in Virginia— nor any among the Indians—that mules or ammunition were turning up. Larabee knew his work well. If Indians had made that raid, he would have found some evidence. If an organized gang had taken it, they would have sold both the mules and the ammunition as soon as possible. No gang Larabee knew about had any way of hiding Army supplies while they waited for a top price offer. Their way was to grab, run, and sell.

Larabee rode on slowly, searching and finding nothing. He swore again. This was the fourth such raid in a little over a year. And like the others, he was forced to follow a cold trail here. He stopped at the mouth of the left-side canyon. Here, if the surviving soldier could be

3

believed, the raiders had appeared.

It had happened in early June with the spring mud still lying thick and clinging. The long train of wagons and mules made slow progress through the Big Hole and even slower when they got to this canyon. The Cavalrymen, dressed as mule skinners and drovers, tried to push their animals to more speed. Dusk was coming and they wanted to be through the narrow, high-walled canyon and close to Glory Hole before dark.

A short way ahead of the canyon mouth where the raiders suddenly showed, the trail made a sharp bend. Because of the three previous raids, the wagons carrying the guns and other supplies were in one string and the mules, loaded with disguised boxes of ammunition, were in another some distance back. Five men rode with the mules: one man in the lead, two at drag, and the other two on the flanks when the trail was wide enough.

As Larabee built the story from the official reports, the mule string was still between the two canyon mouths when the last wagon disappeared around the bend in the trail.

The lead rider glanced back to check the progress of the mules as they slogged through the chewed-up mud. He didn't like this place. The narrow, high canyon walls gave him a squeezed-in feeling, and he was pleased to see the second drag rider pass the gulch coming in from the right. They weren't making bad time.

Then he turned forward again, and there were the raiders. Two of them rode from the mouth of the left-side canyon, rifles raised and aimed. A shot cut the lead man's horse out from under him and he smashed to the ground. He rolled over and came to his knees in time to see the other four Calvarymen get their guns up. But they were too slow. The pair at the canyon mouth shot the two riding flank and guns cracking from the canyon rim above took care of the ones riding drag.

Before the mules could even think about breaking into a panic, more riders poured from the two gulches and took charge of the string. The lead man made the mistake of going for the carbine still on his dead horse. A bullet smashed into his side. He went down into the black mud thinking, *This is a hell of a place to die.*

When the shots echoed from behind, the captain in charge of the wagon train swung his horse from alongside the lead wagon and signaled for men to follow him. He came around the bend with a lieutenant hard on his heels. Both reined up, staring in disbelief. Except for the motionless bodies of five men and a lone horse, the trail was empty.

The captain swung in the saddle. 'Get the men moving!' he ordered. 'Run them into those gulches. A string of mules can't have got very far. Move, man, move!'

And so, Larabee thought bitterly, the

5

soldiers had hammered their horses into the gulches. They found nothing but a maze of side canyons, some leading to dead ends, some back to where they'd started. And they'd managed to chew up any useful sign the raiders and the mule train might have left.

At least, Larabee thought, the captain had had sense enough to find that one soldier was still alive and get him to the doctor in Glory Hole. The soldier's story had given the Army the only eye witness account it had of the raid. And, Larabee admitted, considering how little information the Army had to go on, they'd done everything possible.

Because he'd been down with the southern Shosones, trying to find the source of some late-model guns the Indians had acquired, Fort Hall had no choice but to send a Pinkerton man to check out the country until Larabee was free to come.

As the colonel put it, 'Frankly, Major, I hope we aren't wasting Government money. But since you're the only special services man Washington will let me have, I had no choice but to use a Pinkerton.'

And he would be waiting up in Glory Hole, Larabee thought now. There was even a kind of password so that he and Larabee would know one another. Larabee just hoped it wasn't all foolishness, that the Pinkerton man had managed to learn something useful since June.

Larabee slapped the chestnut on the neck. 'Let's ride,' he said. 'There's nothing more to see here.'

The chestnut nickered. Larabee rounded the bend and saw a piece of sky in the distance, at the end of a long slope that started some way along. Larabee said, 'Once on top, we'll have only a half hour's ride to this town of Glory Hole. I hear they've got a fancy hotel with a stable right behind. We can both put on the feedbag.'

The chestnut's nicker was more eager now. Chuckling, Larabee urged it with his heels. The way he rode, slouched in the saddle, he might have been any drifting cowhand trying to reach a settlement by dark. But a closer look said that here was no ordinary drifter, but a man of substance. His fancy California pants, silver chased boots and vest and saddle—they all cried money. In his work, he had long ago learned that to play the role of a poor cowhand seldom gained him much. But to claim to be a ranch owner, a man of property, meant being able to talk with equal ease to the banker or the rancher, or the cowpoke. And he had learned too that it was usually the men with money and power who wanted more of both. And so they were the ones he interested himself in.

He started up the slope, idly wondering what it would be like to just be himself again. To be once more in uniform, to command a

7

body of troops, instead of playing the role of Indian trader or, as now, a ranch owner looking for new land, or a prospector, or any one of the dozen people he had to become these past years as an undercover agent seeking ways to help stem the rising tide of Indian troubles throughout this northwestern part of the country.

He grinned a little at his fancies. 'We wouldn't really like it much,' he told the chestnut. 'A ranch, maybe, when the country is peaceable again.' His grin faded as he added, 'But a lot of hell-fire is going to bust loose before that time comes.'

The chestnut nickered again, but now with a shrill note. Larabee lifted his head and reined the horse in abruptly. He was no longer alone on this trail. Less than a dozen yards upslope, a pair of riders had him blocked from passing. Their horses were still, held on tight reins, as the men stared down at Larabee.

He stifled a sigh, guessing what might be coming. He had seen their kind all over the West: the rough, nondescript clothing, the faces needing a shave, the teeth needing a dentist's hand. Their gear was old and worn, but the guns they wore low down and ready for drawing had a serviceable, well used look about them. And on their faces he saw the thought: *Here's a pilgrim ripe for some fun, for a good hoorawing.*

And yet somehow he couldn't quite believe

those expressions. Not from this hard-bitten pair.

The bigger man grinned suddenly, showing two broken teeth and one missing. 'You,' he said roughly. 'Where do you think you're going?'

Larabee raised his right hand slowly and ran his thumb along the line of his lean jaw. 'If it's any of your affair, I'm heading for the town of Glory Hole.'

'It's my affair,' the man said. 'This is Barling's land.'

'And you're Barling?' Larabee queried. His voice was soft, deceptively pleasant.

'We work for him,' the man said. 'And this is his trail. The one you're supposed to be on runs north of here.'

'My map says this is the cutoff road that leads over into Idaho Territory,' Larabee answered with the same softness. His thumb kept massaging his jaw.

'It was until this summer when Barling leased all this land from the Government,' the man said.

'I must have missed Barling's "keep-off-this-land" sign,' Larabee said dryly. 'Give him my apologies.'

'It ain't that easy,' the rough-voiced man said. 'There's been too much Lazy B stock butchered lately to let you drifters ride free and easy around here and help yourselves to a free beefsteak.' He leaned forward in the

9

saddle, thrusting his heavy face at Larabee. 'Or maybe you got some other reason for taking this trail?'

'I do all my eating in towns,' Larabee said, still pleasantly. 'And maybe I took this trail because I like riding down into canyons. Now move aside. My belly says it's supper-time.'

The other man, silent up until now, spoke in a thin, nasal voice. 'Maybe we better take him along and find out what he's doing down here, Dirk.'

'I was thinking the same,' the bigger man answered.

Larabee continued to scratch his jaw. As always when faced with a long ride, he wore his gun in a tied-down, clip-spring shoulder holster with his vest loose over it. Now, with his right hand up and his left lightly holding the reins, he was ready to put to use the maneuver he'd learned well over the years. His left hand lifted, flicking aside his vest. His right hand dropped from his jaw, the fingers closing over the butt of his gun. A jerk and it came free of the clip-spring holster and swung up. The muzzle of his .44 was lined on the pair before they could think about reaching for their own guns.

'I tried to be polite, gents,' Larabee said softly. 'Now just move those horses out of my way—fast!'

Dirk laughed. 'You got no sense of humor, friend. We was just hoorawing you a little.

10

Ain't that right, Briggs?'

'Sure,' Briggs answered. 'We was just having us some fun—to pass the time, like.'

'The fun is all mine now,' Larabee said. 'Ride past me, and keep your reins high, with both hands.'

Dirk glowered at him, his face turning a muddy color with the rage working inside him. Then he started his horse forward, hands holding the reins up by his face as he'd been ordered. Briggs followed closely.

At the foot of the slope, they stopped and turned. Larabee sat turned toward them, watching, not moving. They swung around and rode on, sending their horses out of sight beyond the bend.

Now Larabee turned and urged the chestnut up the slope and into the open. A quarter of a mile along, he glanced back to see them appear at the top of the canyon. They looked his way, and then they turned south and disappeared. Holstering his gun, Larabee hurried the chestnut through the gathering dusk.

Larabee's mind turned over what the pair back there had said. Why would this Barling—whoever he might be—lease a useless sprawl of chopped up land like this? And why would he then go to the expense of dragging out a new trail when the old one seemed to go nowhere near grazing country?

Larabee was still mulling over the problem

when he topped a low rise and saw the evening
lights of Glory Hole ahead.

CHAPTER TWO

Despite its name, Glory Hole was built on beef, not on nuggets. It lay in a cup of the Bitterroot mountains, a grassy basin that was a kind of appendage to the Big Hole.

Larabee had the story of the naming of the town and the land from the two friendly local men who stood near him at the hotel's saloon-bar. The taller of the pair did most of the talking. In answer to Larabee's wondering aloud about the name, he said, 'Some six years back, just about this time, a cattleman was driving a herd over the mountains to Alder Gulch. An early fall storm pushed him off the trail and he ran his cows into the nearest timber he could find. A chinook finally came up and ate away the snow. When the cattleman rode out of that timber, he found this big cup of grass belly high to a long-legged horse.

' "Glory be!" he shouted. "To the devil with driving these here cattle to them miners. I'm staying right in this hole!"

'His cowhands started calling it Glory Be Hole. That got shortened to Glory Hole, and that's the way it stayed.'

The man chuckled and showed fine, white teeth under a line of dark moustache. 'And I know that for a true story because my father and I came in on his heels with three loaded wagons and set up a mercantile just a block down from where we stand now.'

He stepped toward Larabee, his hand extended. 'I'm Brooks Reardon. Welcome to Glory Hole.' He nodded to his shorter, stouter companion. 'Dan Peters, who came four months ago for his health and stayed to open a law office.'

Larabee shook hands and gave his name. He was most interested in Peters, the man who had not come here until after the raid on the mule train.

Larabee said, 'This cattleman who got caught in the storm—his name wouldn't have been Barling?'

Surprise flickered over Reardon's finely chiseled features. 'Now that's a strange question. If you know Barling, you'd be aware he didn't come here until three years back. If you don't know him, why would his name come to your mind?'

'That might not be a fair question to ask the witness,' Peters said lightly. In the last few moments, he had changed from a quiet withdrawn man to one who had all the appearance of having been dealt at least four aces. He smiled engagingly at Larabee. 'Brooks isn't as nosy as he sounds, Mr. Larabee. But he is interested in anyone who comes here. He's hoping to get you to stop long enough to invest in Glory Hole.'

Larabee sipped his whiskey. 'No offense taken. As for Barling, I heard the name for the first time a little over an hour ago. I was coming through the canyon-land on the old trail when two of his men blocked the trail and tried to hooraw me a little.' He added casually, 'They called each other Dirk and Briggs.'

A cloud passed over Reardon's face. 'Those two!' He turned on Peters. 'The next time they start a roughhouse down at the Cattleman's Saloon and get thrown in jail, leave them there.' He said to Larabee. 'Since Peters came here, he's had to get that pair out of jail four times.'

'Five,' Peters said. 'Once when you were away on business.' He shrugged. 'I'm a lawyer. If they ask for my services, I can't very well refuse.'

Larabee had the feeling that despite the surface friendliness between Reardon and Peters, underneath there ran a layer of antagonism. And, he thought, their interest in him was more than a passing stranger warranted.

He said, 'They both looked like the kind who'd enjoy a fight.'

Reardon nodded. 'So they do. But don't be taken in by what they might have said. They're a couple of miners from the hills to the south. They only work for Barling when he needs extra hands and they need a grubstake.'

He let his teeth show again in a smile. 'Since

15

you're here and unmarked, I assume their hoorawing didn't come off too well.'

'No,' Larabee said, 'it didn't.' He added casually, 'Back in Wyoming, they've got hoorawing down to a fine art.'

'Ah,' Reardon said. 'You're from Wyoming then?'

'All the way from,' Larabee said. 'I sold my spread there and now I'm looking for country where the wind doesn't peel the hide off the cows.'

He saw by Reardon's expression that he had risen another notch in the man's estimation. Here was a man who obviously had money and who was looking for a place to spend it.

Larabee said, 'Like that first cattleman you spoke about, this place looks pretty nice to me.'

He sipped his whiskey and waited, wondering if Peters was the man he wanted. He suspected as much, and when Peters said, 'Montana isn't famous for its warm winters—not even the Glory Hole,' then Larabee knew he was right. He finished his drink, trying to think of the best way to get a message to the man.

'The heavy winters make the grass grow tall,' Reardon said. 'And there's a lot of fine native hay meadow around. You could do worse than look at the Glory Hole.' He chuckled. 'Of course, all the land is taken right now, but you might find someone interested in going partners.'

'I just might ride around and have a look-see for the next few days,' Larabee said.

Peters said quickly, 'Come to my office tomorrow then. I have the latest map of the area.'

Before Larabee could more than nod, the tired-looking aging desk clerk came up to Reardon. 'Miss Graham would like to see you when you aren't busy.'

'Thanks, Finley. Tell her I'll be right along.' Reardon turned to Larabee. 'Don't forget to try the dining room. It's the best north of San Francisco.'

Larabee watched him go. The bartender moved away to serve another customer, and Larabee said softly to Peters, 'Come to my room when you can. First on the left at the top of the stairs.'

Peters nodded. 'By ten o'clock. Things will be quiet then.' He raised his voice as the bartender drifted back toward them. 'Brooks wasn't boasting, even if he is half owner of this hotel. It is a fine dining room.'

'With all that praise, I'm ready to sample it,' Larabee said. He went out into the lobby and started for the dining room on the far side. Reardon and a tall, fine looking young woman were standing just inside the doorway.

Reardon said, 'Ah, Larabee. Miss Graham, may I present Mr. Larabee, a rancher from Wyoming. I'm trying to convince him he should buy into some Glory Hole cattle land.'

She held her hand out to Larabee, laughing. 'I'm surprised that Brooks didn't try to sell you some of the town real estate he owns—or a piece of his bank.'

'He'd be wasting his breath,' Larabee said. 'I've lived in the open too long to stand being cooped up in a town.' With a nod and a final admiring glance at the girl, he moved on into the dining room. She was more than handsome, he thought. She was on the edge of being beautiful—tall and slim figured, with dark blond hair setting off smoke-gray eyes and a skin with just enough tan to it to show that she had no fear of facing the wind and sun. He wondered if she was Reardon's woman.

Later, he asked Peters the question. Tired from his long day's ride, he was dozing on the bed when Peters knocked at his door. He let the man in and then went to the wash-basin to douse his face in cold water.

'Sorry I took so long,' Peters said, 'but Lynn—Miss Graham, that is—wanted to go over some business contracts with me.'

'Business? Is she associated with Reardon?' Larabee went back to stretch out on the bed. He began to fill his pipe.

'They're equal partners in this hotel,' Peters said. 'Lynn came here less than two years ago, talked Reardon into investing his money in the ramshackle hotel that stood here. Her efforts

18

have turned it into as fine a place as a man could find in these parts.'

Larabee looked around the comfortable, well appointed room. 'Finer than most I've seen around,' he agreed. 'I'd say that Reardon is a lucky man.'

'Don't misunderstand,' Peters said quickly. 'There's nothing between Brooks and Lynn but business. I'm the one she's engaged to marry.'

Larabee struck a match and held the flame to his pipe. 'You don't cotton too much to Reardon, do you?'

'If you mean, I'm jealous—the answer is no. But you're right. He doesn't set too well with me. He's a man with a driving urge to double the fortune his father left him. And I don't trust a money hungry man who smiles too much.'

He shrugged. 'But that's neither here nor there. You want to know what I've learned about the raid these past four months.'

'It was in my mind,' Larabee agreed dryly.

Peters said sourly, 'Nothing. It was the talk of the town when I came here, so I had a good excuse to ride out and look over the place where it happened. Then since I supposedly came for my health, I had reason to do a lot of riding. I scoured the entire area—all the canyons, even the near part of the mountains. I found no more than the Army men who came shortly after the raid—nothing.'

19

'Just tell me everything you can remember hearing, and seeing,' Larabee said. 'Let me judge how much it's worth.' He puffed on his pipe. 'Right now, I don't even know the way you work. I've never teamed with a Pinkerton man before, and I know nothing about you.'

'Meaning that you aren't sure I've been handling my end?' Peters queried.

'I'll reserve judgment on that too.'

'Just remember,' Peters said stiffly, 'that Pinkerton started during the war. The Government used his men to root out Cooperheads and other organizations like it. They did a good job, good enough to still be used now and then. I was too young to work for them during the war, but I've been at it these past five years. I think I know my business.'

'Don't get your hackles up,' Larabee said. 'You did fine with that password about the winter weather and having me come to your office to look at a map. It was quick thinking.'

Some of the feistiness left Peters. 'That password's about all the information I've been given. Oh, I know about you and your work, but I know almost nothing about this last series of raids. Not even exactly what I'm looking for—except a string of mules.'

'Thirty mules loaded with boxes of ammunition disguised as sacks of flour,' Larabee said. 'That's all they took in this raid. They got cartridges for the new Model 1873

Springfields—and that means .45-55-405 shells for the carbines and .45-70-405's for the Long Tom's. And they got .56-50's for the seven shot Indian model Spencers, and .44 caliber shells for the Henry's and the new model Winchesters. In other words, they took ammunition to fit every type of gun they stole in the earlier raids. All told, the raiders have helped themselves to enough Government guns and ammunition to outfit a fair-sized army—and a lot of Indians.'

'But if they'd sold any of it to the Indians, someone would know,' Peters said.

Larabee nodded. 'It's being held somewhere. My guess is that whoever runs those raiders figured out a way to get top price for what they took. He's got a central cache someplace, where it's all stacked and waiting for trouble to start. And he'll hold the guns and the shells until the Indians have to have them. Then he'll sell—at his own price.'

Peters frowned. 'And you think one gang made all the raids?'

'All those we haven't solved,' Larabee agreed. 'And a gang of white men, not Indians. Every raid has gone the same way. The raiders knew just where the supply trains were going to be at a certain time. They knew the best time and place to make their hits. And they were well organized, well drilled.'

Peters nodded. 'You think too that there's going to be real trouble soon? That the raiders can afford to hold what they took so they can get a higher price later?'

'I know there'll be trouble,' Larabee said flatly. 'The Sioux are about pushed over the edge east of us. The Shosone to the south and the Blackfeet to the north haven't been able to trust their treaties with the Government. And the Nez Percé west of us aren't very happy either. I think the fuse has already been lit—and Washington struck the match.'

'That's strange talk coming from a cavalry officer.'

'The Indians have a case on their side,' Larabee said. 'I've lived among them off and on for quite a few years now. I've seen how much the treaties are worth. I've seen what happened after ranches and wagon trains have been attacked too. So there's provocation on both sides. I'm not defending the Indians, but I can't defend Washington either—not when they know they'll break a promise as soon as they make it.'

He lit another match for his pipe. 'I've said my piece. Now you say yours.' When Peters merely spread his hands, Larabee said, 'Let's start with the people who came here a little before the time of the raid, and those whose business takes them into the mountains to the south and west.'

Peters grimaced. 'That's the way I started in on the problem. I found out that Dirk Kessler and his crew came to the Glory Hole country in May, about the time the snow began to go out of the lower part of the mountains. Everybody thought they were crazy for hunting gold up there, but after a while they came down with a few pokes of nuggets and a lot of talk about being close to the mother lode.'

'Where in the mountains was their camp?' Larabee demanded.

'Up behind Barling's home place and west a ways; about due south, in fact, of the chopped up country.' Peters took a slim cigar from his pocket and moistened the tapered end. 'And the camp is still there, along with most of Dirk Kessler's crew.'

He continued to moisten the cigar. 'But don't get your hopes up, Larabee. It's what I did. Kessler and his outfit look like they should be the raiders. Only they aren't.'

Larabee blew a smoke ring. 'You mean they don't seem to be, on the surface.'

Peters shook his head stubbornly. 'The Army boys scoured the whole countryside around their camp. They didn't find anything suspicious. I did some looking around myself. Kessler and his men are just what they claim to be—miners.'

'Just how much mining really goes on?'

'Enough so that they bring in some color now and then,' Peters said. 'They had a dry spell this summer when they started tunneling into a cliff. Kessler came to town with a story about being closer than ever to the mother lode. Most people paid no attention, but he

23

must have had something to show. Brooks Reardon is a pretty shrewd businessman and he went up, took a look, and then grubstaked Kessler for a couple of months.'

Larabee grunted. 'What about Barling? It strikes me odd that he'd be concerned about a traveler riding through that useless country just because he has a lease on it. And why did he go to the trouble and expense of closing the old trail and building a new one?'

'You can forget Barling too,' Peters said. 'In the first place, he doesn't own the Lazy B. Miss Graham does. She bought it from him last winter and he just acts as a kind of ramrod-manager for her. It was her idea to lease the land so she could get more hay meadow. She had to take the canyons along with the other. As for her building a new trail, she did it because the old one is choked with snow too much of the year. She's a fine businesswoman, Larabee. She thinks of everything when it comes to making an honest dollar. She figured that the easier it was to travel to or through Glory Hole, the better off the town—and the hotel—would be. She's right, of course.'

'That doesn't explain Dirk Kessler and Briggs stopping me down in the canyon,' Larabee said. 'And they claimed to work for Barling.'

'They did—at roundup. They don't now. My guess is that they're the ones who've been helping themselves to Lazy B beef and they're afraid Lynn—or Barling, since most people think he still owns the ranch—might have called in some range law.'

'All right,' Larabee said dryly, 'so you managed to eliminate everybody and every place around here. That doesn't leave much to go on.'

'You seem convinced that those mules and the ammunition are still in these parts,' Peters said.

'They have to be—waiting for the right time to be moved to the central cache,' Larabee replied. 'And that can't be too far off. Somewhere over the mountains in Idaho Territory or in this part of Montana is about as central a place as you can get for reaching the most war-like tribes.'

He took time to relight his pipe. 'We know that no string of thirty mules has come out of the mountains or gone across them into Idaho since the raid. The Cavalry has every usable trail watched. And they've scoured the whole area south and west of us as well as they've been able.' He frowned. 'The trouble is—how do you hunt through a country that's only half mapped? How do you scout canyons that you don't know exist?'

Peters said, 'You make it sound as hopeless as I feel.'

'No,' Larabee argued. 'I see it this way. Somewhere close by those mules are hidden. If I can find out where—and who has them—

then I can squeeze down and make the raiders run for the central cache. With luck, I can follow.'

'If they have got the mules in the mountains, they'll have to move them soon anyway,' Peters said. 'Winter in these parts doesn't make for much traveling. But where do you start looking?'

'Where you left off,' Larabee said. 'In the canyons where the raid took place.'

Peters stood up and moved toward the door, his cigar still unlit. 'And my job?'

'Sit tight and play lawyer until I call for help.'

Peters nodded. 'One warning, Larabee. Watch out for Dirk Kessler. He's mean. And if you riled him, he'll do anything to get back at you—any way he can.'

'I riled him,' Larabee admitted. He rose to let Peters out.

CHAPTER THREE

After Peters left Lynn Graham shortly past ten o'clock, Reardon went to her office. 'Larabee is thinking of buying into a ranch in the Glory Hole.'

Lynn looked up from some papers she was studying. 'And I just might be interested,' she admitted. She tapped a sheet of figures lying faceup on her desktop. 'I'm afraid the Lazy B hasn't brought me the profits I've expected. Either this spring's calf drop was awfully low or someone helped themselves to a half herd of calves as well as about two dozen steers ready for market.'

Reardon frowned. 'You don't think Barling is picking up a little on the side?'

'I think I'm a fair judge of character,' she retorted. 'And I wouldn't have left him in charge if I thought he was capable of that sort of thing.' She looked away from the sheet of figures and directly at Reardon.

'Why don't you get to the point, Brooks?'

He spread his hands. 'All right. You're going to marry Dan one of these days. His law business won't keep him so busy that he can't do some of the work around here too—the kind of work I'm doing now. And frankly, I'm not too enamored with the hotel business. I find it takes too much of my time from the

27

bank and the mercantile. And as you know, I want to run for the Territorial Legislature at the next election.'

'In other words, you want to sell your share of the hotel,' she said in her direct way. She added, 'Do you need cash badly right now, Brooks?'

'Why, no,' he said quickly. 'But frankly, I'd like to put my money into something that will yield a profit faster. I know this is safe and steady—but it is a bit slow.'

'With my investment in the Lazy B and my losses this year . . .' she began. She stopped and shook her head. 'So that's why you mentioned Larabee to me! You think that he might buy into the ranch and leave me with some ready cash.'

'It was in my mind,' he admitted dryly.

'Sometimes I think you're almost a rogue,' she murmured. 'I'm glad you're my partner and not my business enemy. I wouldn't like you as an enemy, Brooks.'

'Nor I you,' he admitted.

'If I do sell a share in the Lazy B, I'll buy out your interest in the hotel,' she agreed. 'That is, if there's enough cash involved.' She laughed. 'There, now it's up to you to sell Larabee on the idea—and the more he offers, the more chance you have of getting the cash you want.'

Reardon smiled. 'As your banker, I think I'll charge you a commission too, if I handle the sale.'

She joined in his laughter and they settled down to working companionably on some hotel problems. It was close to eleven o'clock when Reardon, tapping away a yawn, rose and left. Finley, the clerk, was dozing behind the hotel desk. The lobby was empty. In the quiet, Reardon's ear caught the soft closing of the door at the top of the stairs. Since Larabee's room was there, Reardon's interest quickened.

He hurried softly up the carpeted staircase. He was in time to see Dan Peters unlocking his own door and going into the room. 'Well, well,' Reardon murmured softly. 'So Peters and Larabee have been having a visit.'

What business, he wondered, could be so important between them that a man who had ridden all day would stay up so late to discuss? He turned the possible answers over in his mind, and the one that seemed most plausible was the one he disliked the most. Waiting no longer, he hurried downstairs and outside.

He paused on the board sidewalk and surveyed the quiet main street. Only a few bits of light splashed through windows and onto the dusty roadway light from the Cattleman's and Glory Be saloons, from the hotel, from the marshal's office. Otherwise, Glory Hole was asleep until early morning.

He crossed the wide street that ran past the side of the hotel and on up to the town's better homes at the foot of the enclosing hills. His bank was on the opposite corner and he stopped outside it for a moment, frowning as his thoughts turned back to his talk with Lynn Graham. He chuckled sourly. She had touched a sore spot when she'd asked if he needed cash badly. He would have to be careful, he thought, just how he spoke around her. Lynn was too shrewd not to guess he was in trouble—if he said the wrong thing to her.

He swore as he went on down the street toward the Cattleman's Saloon. He would be all right financially if that fool railroad would make up its mind and start building across Montana. He had paid well for a secret copy of their planned route and for the information that they would begin buying up land for rights-of-way in those areas where they couldn't get Government land for nothing. He knew he had taken a risk in taking options on that right-of-way land in a dozen places—and he had paid well for them to keep the transactions secret. But then a chance to make a fortune so easily didn't come to a man too often.

He swore again. All this was history now, of course, because shortly after he'd closed his last deal—a little over a year and a half ago— the railroad had decided they would build only after the Indian troubles were more settled. On first hearing the news, Reardon had known fear for the first time in his life. He had invested heavily, using bank funds—investors' money. And within the coming year, he would have to pick up the options on the lands he had bought or lose all that he had gambled.

After his first panic, he settled down and thought through his problem. Then he made two moves. He traveled to San Francisco where he arranged to borrow on his Glory Hole real estate. With that money, he was able to build back the bank's reserves. Then he scoured the gold camps in Montana until he found the man he wanted—Dirk Kessler. And with him Reardon made another kind of deal.

He was looking for Kessler now, and he found him, as he'd hoped, in the Cattleman's. He was playing poker with four other men and he glanced up when Reardon came in and took a place at the bar. No one showed surprise at Reardon's being there. Since his return from the East when he'd inherited his father's holdings, he had had a thought to politics, and he'd made it a point to spend some time each week in all the places where he could meet and talk with people.

He ordered beer and moved his glass in apparent aimlessness along the bar. A glance in the bar mirror showed him that Dirk Kessler was watching and had got his message. Chatting desultorily with the bartender, he finished his beer, called a good night, and went out. He walked up to his home at the foot of the hill cupping the south edge of the town, lit lamps in his study, and settled down with a cigar to wait.

Kessler came in soon, using the side door that opened to the garden. He moved quickly and softly for a big man. He padded across the room and helped himself to a drink of whiskey at Reardon's private bar, and to a cigar from his humidor.

'I figured it was about time for us to get together,' he said. 'Winter ain't far off. We got to think about moving that string of mules down to the cache.'

'That's one of the things on my mind,' Reardon admitted. 'The other is Larabee.'

'Who?'

'The man you tried to hooraw in the canyon this afternoon. What was the point of that?'

'I don't like to see people snooping down there,' Kessler growled. 'And this joker spent a long time staring around where we made the hit. I know, because Briggs and me laid on the rim and watched him.'

Reardon nodded to show his lack of surprise. 'Somehow,' he said, 'I don't trust our Mr. Larabee. He drifted in with a story about being a Wyoming rancher who'd sold out because he wanted a better climate to raise cows in. Then he takes a sudden fancy to this country and talks about buying here. Besides that, there's something under that easygoing surface he shows—something I can't put my finger on.'

'I can,' Kessler said flatly. 'I got a smile from him too—with a lot of ice under it. And he

32

outdrew me like I was a wet-nosed kid. He didn't learn that kind of draw nor to carry his gun in a spring-clip shoulder holster by raising cows in Wyoming—or anyplace else.'

He studied Reardon over his whiskey glass. 'You think he's dangerous enough to take care of? Like an Army snooper, maybe?'

'He just might be,' Reardon admitted. 'But don't try rousting him just yet. He's going to ride around and look over the country—so he says. Follow him and see where he goes and what he's most interested in.'

He paused and added, 'I want Peters watched too. He and Larabee had a private visit tonight in Larabee's room.'

'I might be able to do better than watching him and trying to guess what he's up to,' Kessler said. 'That new man I got last week saw Peters the other day and thinks he's something besides what he claims to be. I packed him off—Farley's his name—to Alder and Helena to do some asking around. This ain't no time to take risks.'

'No,' Reardon agreed. 'I'm pretty sure that when spring comes, we'll be able to move the guns and ammunition at top prices.'

'You paid enough people enough money,' Kessler said softly. 'They should earn what they got and get them Indians stirred up even faster than they would be anyway.'

'Where did you hear that?' Reardon demanded sharply.

Kessler downed his whiskey and helped himself to more. 'You think I'm a fool, Reardon? I didn't take up your offer to make them raids for you just on the hope you'd pay me someday.' He shook his head. 'Hell, I was making a good living with my boys rustling a herd here and there, stealing this gold shipment or that one. But I saw my chance to make real money after talking to you—the kind of money that'll buy me a nice spread so's I can settle down and live easy. I didn't figure on risking that by going in with you blind.' He laughed. 'You might say I bought myself some insurance. I did a little checking on you.'

'How?' Reardon masked his anger, knowing he had to have Kessler's help for at least long enough to get the ammunition to the cache.

'Why, I just went into that tin can bank of yours and had me a long look-see at them papers you keep locked up so private. They told me a lot: like how much money you borrowed from the bank to buy that right-of-way land and how much you're going to owe the blood-suckers in San Francisco if you can't pay off the loans they made you.' He laughed again. 'Hell, Reardon, if we don't do good business from the raids, you'll lose the whole town of Glory Hole to them.'

'What are you leading up to?'

'Just that our sixty-thirty deal don't set too well no more. You may have laid out the money to keep me and the boys through the summer and found us a buyer for the Lazy B stock we stole, and you may have paid out plenty to them Army men to let you know just when and where the supply trains was going to be. But me and my boys did the dangerous work. So now, with my insurance, I'm figuring on a fifty-fifty split.'

'To the devil with you!'

Kessler showed his broken teeth in a wide grin. 'Think it over. Meanwhile, don't get no ideas about me. I write a pretty good hand and I copied a lot of that stuff. I got it put where if anything happens to me, it'll go to interested people—like the Banker's Association and the U.S. Army.'

He rose. 'When we finish our deal, I'll give it all back to you.' He grinned again. 'Meantime, I'll keep an eye on Larabee and Peters. And if this Larabee turns out to be a snoop—I'll take care of him.' Taking another cigar, he slipped out the way he had come in.

CHAPTER FOUR

With a rough copy of Peters' map in his pocket, Larabee rode out of Glory Hole to look over the countryside. It was in his mind to go first to the Lazy B and so he went east over the low saddle and back into the chopped up country. In less than a mile of riding, he realized he was being followed.

'Let's do one of your tricks, fellow,' he told the chestnut softly. His hand on the reins gave a short, sharp movement. The chestnut seemed to stumble and then catch itself. It stopped, its right front leg lifted almost clear of the ground.

Larabee dropped out of the saddle and knelt by the lifted leg. He made a thorough show of examining it, moving around as if he was looking from all angles. At each change of position, his head went up a little—enough so that he could look around. He saw them finally—two riders off to the southeast, half outlined against the sky, half blended into the backdrop of the mountains. They were motionless, obviously watching.

Larabee acted as if he had found a small stone in the chestnut's hoof, rose and tossed it aside, patted the horse on the neck, and climbed back into the saddle. It moved forward gingerly, limping a bit the first few steps, but finally settling down to its former easy pace.

'When we retire, I'm going to put you on the stage,' Larabee said. He laughed as he gave the horse another affectionate slap.

The laughter drained away as he considered the possible meaning of the two men behind and to his right. Kessler and Briggs, he was almost certain. He cast his mind back, trying to recall if he had ever run into the pair before. He had spent a fair portion of his working life in these parts, but more on the other side of the Bitterroots, or in them. He shook his head. The chances they knew who he was were slight. Even after he'd finished an assignment, few people involved ever learned his real business. Usually he just faded out of the picture and let the men from the nearest Army post do whatever had to be done.

But that they were suspicious was obvious. At first, he was irritated, thinking that their being behind him would slow up his work. Then he laughed aloud as an idea came to him. Why not give them something to think about? He rode on, planning his next moves as he went.

He rode down into Cold Creek Canyon, reining up just short of the place where the raiders had hit. Leaving the chestnut, he took his hunting knife from his saddlebags and walked to the south canyon wall. Without looking, he was pretty sure that Kessler and

Briggs would be up on the rim observing him. Carefully, he examined the wall and then, with slow and deliberate movements, he worked loose a sample of rock. This he carried to the middle of the trail where the light was better and held it up, studying it from all sides. With a nod, he put the rock in his saddlebag, mounted, and rode on.

When he reached the side gully where the first two raiders had appeared, he turned up it. It was a narrow, deep-walled canyon for a short distance and then it widened enough for the morning sun to strike down on the trail. At a likely place, Larabee stopped and repeated his earlier maneuver. He rode on, noting but not following the innumerable gullies that came into this one. Every now and then he would stop and pick a piece of rock from one of the walls. Sometimes he put it in his saddlebag. Other times, he tossed it aside.

By dinnertime, he began to realize just how twisting this gully was. Now and then he could glimpse the mountains ahead—one time south of him, another to the west. At least twice, he realized, he had doubled back on himself in great S curves. Tired of his game, he turned the chestnut and rode at a steady pace back to Glory Hole.

That afternoon, he made a circuit of the ranches nearest the town, looking over the grazing land and the stock. All the ranchers he met were willing to chat with him but none

38

showed any interest when he talked about buying a share in a spread. He returned to town by suppertime, having learned only one thing of interest.

Later, he mentioned it to Peters. They were having supper together, and Larabee said, 'I talked to a half dozen Glory Hole ranchers this afternoon. None of them has been bothered by rustling this past summer and fall.'

Peters spooned his soup. 'Did you think they had been?'

'According to Kessler yesterday, he was stopping me in the canyon because of all the drifters who'd been helping themselves to Lazy B beef. He claimed I was another one of the same breed.'

'Not enough drifters come through these parts to fill the short end of the Cattleman's bar,' Peters said. 'Kessler was just being himself. I tried to tell you last night—he's a bully boy.'

'There's more than that behind Kessler,' Larabee said. He told Peters about being followed and about his game with the rocks.

Peters chuckled. 'I wonder what Kessler thinks you're up to,' he said. 'I saw him in town a while back. I think I'll drift down to the Cattleman's later and have a listen. That's where he usually hangs out when he's in town.'

'Where does he sleep?'

'Oh, he and Briggs rent an empty room built above the stable behind the hotel here,' Peters said. He smiled. 'Lynn never lets a dollar go by if she can help it.'

The waitress came with their steaks and Larabee waited until she was gone. Then he said, 'Tomorrow I think I'll follow the same pattern. Only I'll work some other canyons—those closer to the foot of the mountains.'

Peters shook his head. 'If you'd kept going up that gully, you'd have got as far into the mountains as any of these canyons will take you,' he said. 'Most of the others dead end considerably short of the hills.'

'It doesn't matter,' Larabee said. 'I want to keep Kessler guessing as well as look over the land itself.'

The next day, he found that Peters was right. He followed a number of other deep cuts through the chopped up landscape, but none took him as close to the mountains as they seemed to promise at first. As before, he spent the morning picking rock from the canyon walls and the afternoon drifting around the other Glory Hole ranches.

The third day, he followed a trail that skirted the west edge of the canyon country. Soon what he took to be a stand of timber on a low hill set against the backdrop of the mountains resolved itself into a scatter of buildings. He found himself crossing an expanse of hay meadow, dotted with well-fed cattle. This, according to his crude map, was the Lazy B.

Kessler and Briggs were still with him, as they had been the two previous days. But they were growing warier, Larabee thought. Only twice had he managed to get a glimpse of them on the second day. And this morning he thought he had seen the pair, but he wasn't willing to swear to it.

When he rode up the hill and around the solid log ranch house to the rear yard, he found a leathery man giving working orders to a half dozen cowhands. He waited until the man was finished and then rode up to him.

'Mr. Barling?'

'I'm Barling.' Old but sharp blue eyes measured Larabee as he got down from the chestnut. 'You must be that Wyoming man I heard about in town last night.'

Larabee gave his name and they shook hands. Then he launched into the story he had built up. Barling ran a thumb along a white stubble of whisker.

'Since you know I don't own this place any more, why come to me?'

'To look over the land and the cows,' Larabee said. He added, 'And to get a few ideas as the best way to approach the lady if I decide to try to buy into the spread.'

Barling laughed and led the way into his big kitchen. He poured out two cups of coffee and took Larabee into his parlor. From there, they could see the rich grassland spread out below and to the west where it folded over hills and

41

down into the main part of Glory Hole. And they could see the canyonlands farther along, with the northern mountains in the hazy distance.

'Good country,' Barling said. 'Even some of that canyon country is better land than it looks. You can't see from here, but between the old trail and the new one, there's a big dish with native hay.'

'The reason Miss Graham leased that land from the Government?' Larabee queried. 'Was that on your advice?'

Barling gave him an odd look. 'Hardly. She isn't one to take advice. She claims that her father tried ranching once along with building and selling hotels.' He laughed. 'She says she learned what to do and what not to do from him. He went broke.' He nodded. 'Everything done here since she bought me out has been on her say-so.'

'Including building a new trail?'

'That too. Of course, she had a reason there: wanting to make winter travel easier.'

'So I heard,' Larabee said. He sipped his coffee and set the mug down while he filled his pipe. 'Was hiring Kessler and Briggs her idea too?'

Again Barling gave him the odd, questioning look. 'Now that's a strange question. What do you know about that pair?'

Larabee told of his meeting with them in the canyon. Barling swore. 'They worked for me during roundup because I was short-handed. They worked off and on in the summer too—for the same reason. But they sure as hell don't work for me, or for Miss Graham now. I sent them packing two weeks back.'

Larabee lifted his eyebrows. 'Kessler looked to me like the kind of man who'd know his way around a ranch.'

'Oh, he knows the work well enough. But him and that Briggs only showed up when they felt like it. Too much salooning at night don't make for a worker the next day. And then every now and again, they'd ride away from the job to go pick at that mine of theirs back in the mountains.'

Larabee wondered if Barling was dodging his question or had forgotten about it. He said through a cloud of pipe smoke, 'Since I've been warned that Kessler might try to get even with me for tricking him on the trail, I'm kind of interested in finding out what sort of man I'm dealing with.'

'Mean and tough and smart. He's a bully, but he's no fool.'

'And willing to work—on his own terms, I gather,' Larabee said. He added casually, 'Did he come to you for a job or did Miss Graham find him in town and send him here?'

Barling scratched his white thatch. 'Come to think of it, the first time him and Briggs worked for me, she'd sent them out. Later, she told me Reardon had suggested them, knowing how short-handed the Lazy B was.'

Larabee nodded and let the subject drop. He talked for a while about cattle and moved the conversation on to rustling. Here, Barling had a good deal to say.

'I know Miss Graham was surprised to find out she hadn't got no profit this year,' he said. 'I was too until I figured out why. This year's the first time since I come here that I've lost a single head to rustlers.'

'You're sure it was rustlers and not cougars or just strayed stock?'

'Sure! Cougars leave a different sign from men. And strayed stock don't drop running irons when they take off. No, by God, it was rustlers all right. After the count, I went out and had a look around. I found plenty of sign that Lazy B stock—steers and weaned calves— had been taken. It'd be easy enough for a small crew to round up a few head at a time, hold them down in one of the canyons, and then some night push the whole lot out of the Glory Hole and away.'

'No ideas as to who did it?'

'I figured it was Kessler's crew of so-called miners,' Barling said. 'But I couldn't find no evidence. And I even went as far as their camp looking around. I reckon it was some outfit from over east that saw a chance for easy pickings.'

'They didn't bother any other spread but

yours, I hear,' Larabee said.

'Mine—or what was mine—is the only one not right down in the Glory Hole itself. It's an easy place to steal from.'

Larabee let the talk drift a while and then took his leave. On his return, he made a swing a short distance into the hills, stopping at two cliffs to gather rock samples, and then rode with apparent aimlessness in the general direction of town. Actually, he was trying to find the big gully that had twisted him back and forth so long that first day. But he soon realized he couldn't tell one canyon from another up above, and he reached the trail and went straight to Glory Hole.

That evening, Peters said, 'Kessler's got the wind up about you, all right. From his talk in the saloon, he thinks you're hunting for gold. He's made a lot of jokes about it, but you can see he's worried.'

'Not about gold,' Larabee said. 'He just can't figure out what I'm up to.' He grinned. 'I think I'll look over the Cattleman's tonight myself. Maybe Kessler'll have something to say to me.'

'Just be sure he doesn't say it with a knife in the back,' Peters warned.

Larabee went to the Cattleman's about an hour after supper. He found Kessler and Briggs at the bar, helping themselves to the free lunch. Kessler was arguing in his rough voice with a frail, very old man about the best places in Montana for a free meal.

'You may be a lawyer, Elston,' he bellowed, 'but you ain't seen the inside of as many saloons as me and Briggs. And I tell you, Helena's got the best food for free in this whole Territory.'

He stopped as Larabee stepped to the bar and ordered whiskey, pointing out the bottle he wanted it poured from. 'Looky here,' Kessler shouted, 'the dude from Wyoming. Hey, Larabee, you expect to find rocks in here?'

Larabee sipped his whiskey and set down the glass. 'No, I came to tell you to get off my back, Kessler. What I do is my own business. The next time I find you following me, you'd better have some cover handy.'

Kessler's unshaven face colored. 'You trying to tell me where I can ride and where I can't?'

'I'm telling you to stop snooping after me!' Larabee made his voice rough, challenging.

He waited for Kessler's reaction. He saw the big man look around at the handful of silent, watchful customers in the saloon. *As if,* Larabee thought, *he's counting his audience.*

Kessler said almost mildly, 'You got something to hide, Larabee?'

'Nothing to hide,' Larabee said. 'And nothing more to say. Just remember—after this, let me ride alone.'

'After this,' Kessler mocked, 'don't come in here—or you won't walk out. You'll be carried.'

CHAPTER FIVE

Larabee spent the following two days drifting around the Hole and making occasional forays into the canyon country. He kept a sharp lookout for Kessler and Briggs, but either they had stopped following him or they were being more careful. He saw no sign of either man.

The second evening, he returned to town, irritated with himself. He had never worked an assignment like this one: no matter where he looked, no matter what questions he asked, he always came up with nothing. He found himself thinking of Peters and of how little the man had managed to learn. His reason told him that Peters had come up against the same unyielding stone cliffs he had found. But he was in no mood to reason, and from the brief moment he spent blaming Peters for wasting time and Government money, an idea began to take shape.

Larabee had always been a careful man in thinking through a problem before he took final action. He had seldom accused the wrong man of doing something, seldom made a mistake in those he had the Army arrest. And so now he stood alone in the hotel saloon, nursing his drink and turning over in his mind this latest idea. His conclusion wasn't a pleasant one, but it made sense.

And as far as he could see there was only one way to find out how close he was to the truth: brace Dan Peters.

He managed to stretch his whiskey until Peters appeared, ready for supper. The last few nights they had made a point of eating together—ostensibly to talk about Larabee's buying a ranch. Tonight they followed the same pattern, discussing the spreads Larabee had visited until the waitress left them alone with their coffee and cigars.

Larabee said bluntly, 'How badly does Miss Graham need money?'

Peters stared at him in surprise. 'Need money? Why should she? The hotel is doing fine, as you can see. If you're thinking about the ranch, she wants to build it up but she plans to do that on her profits. She's never acted as if she was in a hurry.'

Larabee blew a careful smoke ring. 'Barling tells me she lost quite a bit from rustlers this year. She was pretty upset.'

Peters' voice turned sharp. 'Wouldn't you be? She had plans for her profits—and there weren't any.'

Larabee nodded and said softly, 'I understand she bought Barling out in cash and had money enough left over to relocate the trail and to take up the Government lease on all that canyon land. That's a lot of bad country to pay for just to get a hay meadow.'

Peters reached for his coffee cup and jerked his hand back. 'What in the devil are you getting at, Larabee?' His voice lost its sharpness and became ominously soft. 'Just what's on your mind?'

'I was thinking how handy Kessler's being around has been this year—to Miss Graham,' Larabee answered. 'I was thinking that the last places she lived in before she came to Glory Hole weren't too far from where the earlier raids took place, and maybe not too far from where Kessler and his crew hung out. I was thinking that to let someone rustle your stock is one way of paying them for work done for you—without letting people know you are paying them. And I was thinking that leasing that canyonland is one way of keeping people off the old trail, keeping them from snooping too much around where the raids took place. And I wonder if she visited some of those places any time this past year.'

He spoke in a flat, emotionless voice, his eyes fixed on Peters' slowly whitening face. Peters took a slow, deep breath. Then he stood abruptly, his chair crashing over. He leaned down, his hands pushing at the tabletop, his face inches from Larabee's.

'By God, I'd like to hammer those words back down your throat! But I won't cause trouble in Lynn's own hotel. But remember this—from now on, keep out of my way!'

He wheeled around and stalked out, leaving

49

Larabee sitting alone with his cigar and coffee. He saw Lynn Graham come to the door just as Peters reached it. He bowed to her and strode on, obviously too angry to trust himself to speak. With a startled expression on her face, she came to Larabee's table. He rose.

'Whatever happened?' she demanded. 'I've never seen Dan like that before.'

'I ruffled his feathers a mite,' Larabee said. 'Just a misunderstanding. It'll pass, I hope. I like him.'

He offered her a chair but she waved it aside and remained standing. A coy woman, he thought, would have batted her eyes and murmured, 'Was it over me?' But there was nothing coy about Lynn Graham. She said merely, 'I'm sorry. Dan shouldn't get excited. It's not good for his health.' She turned away, leaving him to return to his chair.

He was leaving the dining room when Reardon intercepted him. 'Sorry to be nosy,' he said. 'But—well, this is my town. I dislike hearing that two of its possibly prominent citizens are feuding.'

'I see you've been talking to Miss Graham.'

'I didn't need to. I saw Peters in the bar, tossing down whiskey like a desert rat drinking water.'

'Let's just say I was tactless, and gave him reason to be angry,' Larabee said.

Reardon chuckled, but now with little humor. 'All right, I'll respect your privacy.'

Larabee went on upstairs to his room and lay on the bed, sucking at his pipe and turning over in his mind what had just happened. He hadn't, he admitted sourly, learned very much. But then he hadn't expected to—yet. He looked at his pocket watch and frowned. It was too early to make his next move.

Setting his pipe aside, he dozed for a time. When he awakened, it was to hear footsteps going a bit unsteadily past his door. He rose and quietly looked into the passage. Peters was going to his room at the end of the hall. Larabee waited until he was inside and then followed. Peters opened the door and, when he saw Larabee, tried to shut it again. Larabee's foot and shoulder stopped him. Quickly, Larabee slipped inside and shut the door himself.

'Damn you,' Peters said thickly. Turning, he went for the closet, reached in and grabbed for the gun in the holster hanging on a nail. Larabee snapped, 'Hold it, man. I came to apologize—and to explain.'

Peters drew the gun but kept it pointed at the floor. He walked uncertainly to the bed and sat down. Laying the gun beside him, he ran a hand over his face. 'I'm a little drunk—but not too drunk to listen.'

'First, I was out of line,' Larabee said. 'I was getting desperate, grabbing at anything I could to find an answer to all this.'

Peters merely grunted. Larabee went on,

51

apologizing in the same roundabout way until he saw Peters beginning to relax. Only then did he cross the room and drop into the easy chair.

Peters said suddenly, 'Why don't you come right out and say what's bothering you—that I haven't held my end up? Why don't you tell me that maybe I've let my feelings for Lynn blind me? I didn't investigate her. It never occurred to me.'

'You wouldn't have been much in the way of a prospective husband if it had occurred to you,' Larabee said dryly. 'But I see it has now—and you aren't too sure of her.'

'That's right,' Peters said bleakly. 'And whiskey didn't make thinking about it any easier—one way or the other.' He scrubbed his face with his palm again. 'What the devil do I do now?'

'Don't go to the opposite end and decide she's guilty,' Larabee said sharply. 'Keep an open mind. And help me put a crack in the big blank wall I've run into.'

'I've run out of ideas,' Peters said. He was morose now as the whiskey began to wear off.

'I'm still hanging to one,' Larabee said. 'Those mules disappeared somewhere in the canyon country. The Army hunted all through it and found no trace. But they've also been watching every possible way out of the mountains and the Hole. They know that neither the mules nor the ammunition has got out of this area yet. That means it has to be somewhere in the mountains, and that one of those canyon trails was used to get the mules to wherever they are. It's the only answer that makes sense.'

'I checked out every canyon the raiders could possibly have used. As I said, if they don't twist back on themselves, they're dead ends.'

'I'm going to take one final look,' Larabee said.

'And you want me to go along?'

'No, for the time being let's keep things the way they are: act mad enough to draw on me if you got the chance. We can meet later. When I've got something to say.'

*   *   *

Kessler grunted and came upright, pawing for the gun hanging near his head as a hand clamped down on his shoulder. He blinked when he saw Reardon.

'Hell, it's barely daylight,' Kessler grumbled.

Reardon's nose wrinkled at the smell coming up from the stable directly below. 'It's daylight, all right. And Larabee has already headed for the canyon country. He had the cook pack him enough food for three or four meals. Now, get dressed and after him.' He swung a hand at the rough table across the room. 'I brought you some food. Eat it while you're dressing and keep moving. I don't want

53

Larabee lost, not today.'

'You figure he's on to something?'

'I can't see any other reason for him riding again over country he's been across every day for almost a week.'

'And if he does find anything he shouldn't, you want him killed?'

'No. Not yet. If he is Goverment—or law—I want to learn what made them send a man here after the Army came up empty-handed all summer. I can't learn much with Larabee dead. Just be careful he doesn't see you.'

'That's all—watch and let him look at whatever he wants and then go riding off to report in case he smells something?'

Reardon shook his head. 'Don't be a fool. I'll want him taken care of so he can't go anyplace, but I'll want him left alive. Do you get the idea now?'

Kessler grinned. 'So you heard about me and Larabee nearly having a fight last night? And tonight, or whenever he gets back, you want me to challenge him.'

'I want you to beat him into the hospital. I want him hurt badly enough so that he won't be thinking of doing anything for at least a week. By that time, we can have the mules and ammunition out of these mountains and into the cache. I can smell a hint of snow coming and I want to get started moving tomorrow or the day after.'

'It'll be a pleasure,' Kessler said. 'A real

gen-u-ine plea-sure!'

*   *   *

The good weather was still holding as Larabee rode over the saddle and out of the Glory Hole. He glanced at the horizon and saw nothing threatening. But he knew this country. It could be perfect Indian summer one day and howling winter the next. He was sure that with the pressure of time, the weather and—if he could find something to go on—himself, the raiders would soon be forced to start out of the mountains. And when they did, he had to be in a position to trail them.

That meant that today he had to get his grip on something meaningful. He had to make a crack in the stone cliff that had been blocking him.

He paused twice to check for Kessler and Briggs before he dipped down the old trail into the canyon. He saw no sign of anyone and so he rode straight to the side gully where the raiders had first appeared to the point man of the mule train. He pressed the chestnut whenever the footing permitted. Now and again the sun would angle down on him as it climbed higher in the sky. Finally he was able to see a piece of the sun and so figure out his direction.

He was going almost due southeast, he judged, and now with each twist and turn in the widening gully, he checked to make sure that he didn't lose that sense of direction. Then, when he judged he was heading straight south, the gully made an abrupt turn to the right, taking him west. Ahead on his left, he saw a dark blotch in the rock wall, and he could hear the rising murmur of water.

As he neared the dark blotch he saw that it was a side canyon—the first, he realized suddenly, that he had seen in some time. His hopes rose as he saw the chewed up mud, but then it went on past the canyon mouth. He swore softly, and more angrily when he took a close look at the canyon. It came into this gully all right, but its bottom was close to ten feet above the gully floor. From the way the rock was scarred, it looked to Larabee as if the gully was some kind of wet weather stream that collected water from the rising mountains he could see looming to the south.

He rode on and made an abrupt halt as the gully suddenly ended. He sat the chestnut and stared at the sharp drop-off in front of its forefeet and at the brawling creek rushing past at the foot of that drop-off.

Larabee's hopes rose again. Here was water, the favorite concealment of a man trying to hide his sign from pursuers. From the looks of the chewed up trail, the mules could well have been driven this far. Then, he thought, if they'd been pushed into that stream . . .

Leaving the chestnut, Larabee moved

forward for a better look. For the second time his hope turned to ashes in his mouth. September and even October up to now had been unusually dry. Yet this creek was running full, brawling milky white out of some glacier back in the mountains. And if it was running high now, in the snow melt time of June it would have been completely impassable.

Besides, he saw, there was no break other than the spot where he stood: the water ran through high, straight canyon walls. Even if the mules had been driven into it, they would have had no place to land.

Climbing back into the saddle, Larabee rode as far as the mouth of the canyon. He stopped. The ground all through here had been too thoroughly trampled to account for the hoofprints of a few searching Calvarymen. Only a herd of cattle or horses could have made sign so deep that it had managed to stand up through the summer rains until the Indian summer sun baked it.

Again he left the saddle. He needed only one look to know that cattle had never been close to this place. Here and there he could pick out the distinctiveness of horse and mule prints. And the mule prints had sunk deep, the way a laden pack animal would make them.

The sun was high by this time and Larabee could feel the rumbling of emptiness in his belly. Taking a small packet of bread and meat from his saddlebags, he unwrapped it, unslung his canteen, and squatted down to eat and stare at the canyon mouth.

Ten feet up, he thought. *How in the devil could anyone get a loaded mule to climb ten feet up a rough but steep rock face? How . . .?*

He crammed the last of the food in his mouth and climbed to his feet. Going to the base of the rock where the canyon mouth showed above, he started walking toward the sharp bend ahead, keeping close to the side wall of the gully. His eyes picked over the chopped up dirt until he found what he had been looking for.

And now the hope rose in him and stayed. Because that sharp, three-foot wide straight line standing out at an angle from the side wall could mean only one thing: the end of a wide, thick plank had been sloped down into the ground.

Grinning now, Larabee hurried back to the canyon mouth. He scrambled up the ten feet, using the roughness of the rock to find finger- and toeholds and finally stepping to the canyon floor. He stared down at it, momentarily puzzled. Except for some long, thin ridges of squeezed up, baked mud running lengthwise away from him, the dirt was smooth. No mule, no horse had left his sign here.

They brought the mules and horses up on planks, Larabee thought. *But then what?* He slapped his fist into his palm. Then more planks to hide the fact that the mules had come up this way—in case anyone like himself got curious enough to climb up for a look.

He strode forward. He was going due south now and rising above the high, slick rock walls of this canyon he could see the peaks of the mountains. He covered, he judged, a good thirty feet, and then the canyon made a sharp Z turn.

Larabee laughed aloud. Beyond the Z the sign showed again. Here the long, thin ridges of dirt that must have been squeezed up between the cracks of planks laid down disappeared, and here began the heavy chopped up ground that could only mean that a loaded train of mules and a fair number of horses had passed this way.

The canyon stretched on straight, its bottom lost in shadow as the walls rose higher and higher with the burrowing of the canyon deeper into the mountains. Larabee turned to go back, and now he saw what he had missed on his way in—a stack of planks and coils of rope with metal pins to attach their ends to the rock walls. They lay in dimness, hidden by an undercut in the rock. Larabee spent a moment examining them and then went on.

He returned to the chestnut, mounted, and started back the way he had come. He loped the horse now, formulating his next move as he rode. He was almost within sight of the opening onto the main trail when the sharp crack of a rifle and the whine of lead off the wall ahead made the chestnut shy.

Larabee pulled up and dropped to the ground, drawn carbine in hand in one swift, trained movement. He pressed himself into shadow and peered upward.

He could see nothing, but raucous laughter and a mocking voice came down to him. 'Been for a ride, Larabee?'

Larabee tried to judge the position of the voice so that he could draw a bead. But when it came again, its owner had moved. 'Remember what you told me in the saloon, Larabee? Well, come in tonight and back it up!'

Larabee stepped to the middle of the trail and looked skyward. 'Tonight, Kessler,' he agreed. 'Eight o'clock.'

CHAPTER SIX

Reaching town, Larabee rested for a time and then washed for supper. Going into the bar for his drink, he saw Peters, gave him a quick signal and then pointedly ignored the man. Gulping his drink, Larabee went to the dining room. He ate a light supper, not taking too much time, and then started for his room.

As he started for the stairs, Lynn Graham came from the hallway that led to her office and stopped him. He said politely, 'Good evening, Miss Graham.'

She looked almost beautiful, he thought; a handsome dress molded to her figure and her fine skin highlighted by two spots of color in her cheeks.

The color deepened as she made an obvious effort to say what was on her mind. 'That—that man Kessler is boasting all over town that he's going to fight you tonight!' she burst out.

'So he is,' Larabee agreed.

'And you agreed? Why? What can you gain by fighting a bully like that?'

'Maybe it's in the nature of a man to fight now and then,' Larabee said quietly. 'Or maybe I'm a little dull around the edges and want to hone myself up some.'

'Or maybe you're a plain fool!' she snapped tartly.

'Why should my fighting Kessler concern you, Miss Graham?' He kept his gaze intently on her face, seeking some telltale expression, some indication that the theory he had angered Peters with might have a basis in fact. But he could see nothing but her anger.

'Because it will mean trouble for Glory Hole,' she snapped. 'Kessler isn't a man to take humiliation twice. If you should beat him, you could start a feud. He might bring his miners down from the hills and . . .'

'I don't think Kessler will be in any condition to feud with anyone for some time,' Larabee said dryly. With a polite nod, he stepped around her and went on up the stairs.

He found Peters sitting in the dark, waiting for him. Shutting the door, Larabee checked the window shade to make sure that it was down and then lighted the lamp.

'I found something today,' he said in a low voice. Dropping to the edge of the bed, he began to fill his pipe.

'So did I,' Peters answered. His expression was dour. 'I got to thinking about Lynn—and I admit she had my head turned pretty far. I never really considered her at all before.'

'You admitted as much last night. Forget it.'

'I didn't believe myself then,' Peters said. 'I think I do now. I had a talk with her today— just the way a man will ask questions about his future wife's business experiences and such. She seemed to think it was natural enough, and she didn't try to hide anything.'

'Do you think she might have something worth hiding?'

Peters said with a sour look, 'When those earlier raids happened, she was always away from here—visiting. And each time she was mighty close to where they took place. She even mentioned having known about Kessler before and what a bully he was.'

'It could mean something,' Larabee agreed. 'But then if she had earlier properties to sell, she'd have a reason to travel. Lots of people do in this part of the West.'

'I know,' Peters admitted. 'Brooks had made a number of trips away this year. And in fact, two years back, he stayed in hotels run by Lynn twice when he was away on banking or store business. According to her, his enthusiasm sold her on coming to Glory Hole.'

'All right'—Larabee chuckled—'let's blame it all on Reardon. Now forget Miss Graham for the time being. I found where the mules disappeared to.'

While Peters listened carefully, Larabee sketched out his day and then said, 'It'll take two of us to rig that planking so we can get a horse up into the higher canyon. Then one of us should see where it leads while the other stays on top to see if he can't follow to the end from up above.'

'If Kessler is involved, he wouldn't let you— or me—stay on top for long,' Peters predicted.

'Once he guessed what we were up to, he'd likely start protecting himself.'

'Kessler won't be around to follow anyone,' Larabee said. 'I'm going to see to that in about half an hour.'

'What if he whips you?'

'Then I'll resign my commission and take up sewing,' Larabee said dryly.

Peters grinned but without too much certainty. Larabee said, 'Right now, I've got a few more questions. Did you learn anything about Miss Graham's finances?'

'No mystery,' Peters said. 'She inherited two paying hotels from her father when he died. She sold one and remodeled the other and then sold it at a good price. Then she began— well, roaming. She managed a place in Helena, putting it on its feet, and went on south into Idaho and back north to Alder and around. Finally she came here.' His expression was troubled. 'Right now, she's low. She has almost everything she owns tied up in the ranch. She told me that Reardon wants her to buy out his interest in the hotel but that she doesn't have the cash.'

'Reardon again? What's his problem?'

'He has everything he owns tied up: in inventory at the mercantile, in the hotel, but mostly in land speculation. That's not generally known but old Elston, my law partner, told me in his confidential cups that Reardon has been dealing with a Helena lawyer in getting contract options written up. He's convinced that the railroad is coming through Montana within a year or so and he's been buying what he thinks will be the rights-of-way.'

'I don't know how much all this means,' Larabee said, 'but I'd say you've started earning your pay.' He stood up. 'I'll meet you at midnight over the hill east of town.'

He left quickly and then slowed his pace as he went on down to the Cattleman's. He pushed aside the doors and entered. Kessler's boasting had obviously been for a purpose— the place was crammed with hopeful faces. A sigh rippled through the waiting men as Larabee went up to the bar.

Kessler was there, a drink in his hand. 'All right, I followed you today. What you going to do about it, Larabee?'

A spade-bearded man standing at the end of the bar came forward. 'I'm Dr. McFee,' he said. He shook hands with Larabee. 'The whole town knows about what's going to happen here. I thought you'd like to know that the marshal won't interfere unless there's gunplay or someone breaks up the furniture.'

Larabee nodded to a shotgun that the bartender had laid on the bar. 'I don't figure there'll be any gunplay,' he said. 'As for the furniture, the fight won't last long enough for much to get broken.'

He smiled at the doctor. 'Why are you

here—professionally or just to watch?'

'Both,' McFee said. He pulled a gun from his waistband. 'And to help the bartender make sure no one in the back gets any ideas about changing the way the fight is going.'

Larabee saw that his gaze was fixed on Briggs, standing in the crowd. 'Thanks,' Larabee said. He unbuckled his own gun and belt and laid them on the bar.

'All right, Kessler, unbuckle—and if you're carrying a knife, let's see that too.'

'I don't need no knife to take care of you,' Kessler said. He grinned, showing his missing tooth. Putting his gun and belt aside with a flourish, he grinned again. 'This is going to be a real pleasure, Larabee.'

'I don't know how good you are with your fists,' Larabee said, 'but your mouth makes enough wind to blow me over.'

With a roar of laughter surging around him, Kessler launched himself at Larabee. Both arms were stretched out, his hands doubled into massive fists.

Larabee had had his share of barrack-room fights in his early Cavalry years, and he thought he'd learned every vicious trick in the book. He'd learned too that one good man can't whip another until he knows just how the other is going to fight. So now he watched Kessler warily, looking for a telltale sign of trickery. But all he could see was a lumbering giant with no balance, no grace, no easy

66

muscle movement.

Larabee reasoned that Kessler would be the kind to charge in with roundhouse swings, thinking to beat his man to the ground and then take his time cutting him to shreds. Larabee knew this kind of fighting well and so he stood with his hands hanging limply, waiting for Kessler to make his move.

Kessler stopped his lumbering charge suddenly and launched his left fist in a wild sweeping swing that left his big body and craggy face nakedly exposed. Masking a grin, Larabee stepped in to drive a pair of punches at the big target. As he moved, he ducked to avoid the wild left Kessler was throwing. Larabee caught the flicker of movement coming from the other side, but then it was too late. Kessler had suddenly lost his clumsiness and with both feet moving like a dancer, he had turned his swing into a feint, come around, and now he was smashing his right fist into Larabee's unprotected temple.

Larabee thought dully, *I let him trick me!* He felt his body hurtling sideways, out of control. He felt the thick numbness closing over his mind, darkening the light in the saloon, sending a wild ringing through his ears. His spinning body struck the bar, driving the wind from his lungs but at the same time jarring the mists away from his brain.

For what seemed an endless time, Larabee hung to the bar with one hand, his mouth open as he fought for air. He saw Kessler coming for him, and he knew what would happen if he took too long to regain his strength.

Kessler's grin broadened as he stalked forward, taking his time, making the most of the moment. His quarry was helpless. Now he had gone to one knee and his expression was dulled, lifeless. Kessler ran his tongue over his lips.

'You asked for this, Larabee,' he rumbled. 'All of it.' His foot swung back and then dropped back down. 'Naw,' he said. 'I'd rather beat you to hell.' Reaching down, he stretched one massive paw for Larabee's slack shirtfront. His other arm was cocked back, ready to drive his fist forward when he had Larabee lifted into position.

Larabee let Kessler lift him halfway from the floor, waiting until Kessler's strength was concentrated on pulling his 190 pounds to an upright position. Then Larabee's hanging hands moved, snaking out with the same swiftness he had used going for his gun. Steel trap fingers closed over Kessler's wrist. Larabee's legs thrust him upright the rest of the way and he pivoted in a tight, hard swing. Kessler grunted as he tried to rechannel his strength and resist the momentum Larabee's move slammed into his body. But Larabee's quickness was too much for Kessler. His back slammed painfully against the edge of the bar.

Now Larabee was in front and Kessler was

fighting for breath. But Larabee wasted no time in posing for the crowd. He moved in, fists slashing at Kessler's face and body. He danced back, judging the effects of his blows. Larabee rammed a left to Kessler's chin; he saw no clear effect. He moved in again and rammed two quick fists over Kessler's heart. And now he saw the pain come to the man's face, saw the mist form over his eyes.

That's his weak spot, Larabee said to himself. He started in again. Kessler pushed himself away from the bar and took a swiping swing at Larabee that made him duck away. But now Kessler was moving with painful slowness: his quickness and grace were gone. And Larabee danced around him, chopping at his body, ducking away, coming in again to hit. Larabee's moves were those of a trained fighter and the crowd sensed this. A low swelling murmur began to rise as time after time Larabee swept aside Kessler's feeble defense and scored on the big body.

'Cut him up!' someone yelled from the rear. 'Make mincemeat out of him, Larabee.'

Larabee paid no attention. He aimed every blow at the body, hammering on Kessler's belly, under his heart and over it, driving short, sharp blows to the man's ribs. Kessler was floundering, staggering after the dancing Larabee with a fist cocked as if he hoped to get in the one killing blow.

Then Larabee saw his best opening of the

night, stepped in and crashed both fists viciously to Kessler's side. He felt the man's ribs give. Kessler grunted in pain and turned. Larabee slammed a hard left to Kessler's heart, driving him back to the bar. Kessler was breathing raggedly now, his mouth slack. His face was drained of blood, leaving his skin a dirty yellowish color.

Larabee hit him three times in the belly, three times over the heart. Then he stepped back and waited. Kessler pushed himself toward Larabee, raising his left arm with an obvious effort. Larabee stepped forward and brought his right up under Kessler's breastbone, putting into the blow all the force of his legs and shoulders and muscles.

Kessler made a gagging sound, took one step, and fell on his face.

Dr. McFee was at his side, hands exploring. He looked up, grunting sourly. 'He'll live. But I'm taking him to my hospital. Lord only knows what you broke inside him.' He stood up. 'Briggs, get a couple men to help you pack Kessler to my place.'

Larabee retrieved his gun and belt and started for the door. McFee said, 'You come too, Larabee. You didn't get by clean.'

Larabee lifted a hand to his throbbing temple. It was knotting there and in one place the skin was broken. A thin trickle of blood still ran down his cheek. He nodded and followed McFee out.

He was mildly surprised to find that McFee actually had a kind of hospital—a big room attached to his house. It held four beds and more equipment than Larabee expected to see this far away from a population center.

McFee patched him up. By then Briggs and two men from the saloon had Kessler packed in. McFee had them stretch him on one of the beds and peel off his clothing. He sent Briggs and the others away. 'I'll let you know when I figure out when he'll be coming around.'

When they'd gone, he said to Larabee, 'Why didn't you go for his face? That's what he'd have done to you—marked you for everyone to see how bad a beating he'd given you.'

'His head is like a rock,' Larabee said. 'Why should I break my hands on it? His weakness is his body. There's softness. I found it.

'Send me your bill,' he added, and started out.

'I'll charge it up to Kessler,' McFee said dryly. 'He lost.'

Grinning faintly, Larabee left, crossing the street and walking the half block back to the hotel. He was bone weary and he wanted a rest before he met Dan Peters at midnight.

CHAPTER SEVEN

Reardon had watched the fight and after Briggs left, he lingered briefly at the bar and then went out. He was passing McFee's place, apparently on the way to his own house, when Briggs and the other men came out of the hospital. Reardon brushed against Briggs, his fingers signaling to him as he went on.

A half hour later, Reardon let Briggs into his study through the garden door. He said bluntly, 'Well, the fool let himself get whipped. When can he ride again?'

'The doc didn't say. But Dirk was still out cold when I left.' Briggs looked hopefully at the whiskey on the sideboard.

'Help yourself,' Reardon said. He swore at no one in particular. 'Now listen. See Kessler as early as you can tomorrow. Tell him we've got to get the mules moving. I don't like the way Larabee's been snooping around. I don't like the way he always knew that you and Kessler were trailing him. He's not like any cattleman I ever met.'

'Peters ain't like no other lawyer neither,' Briggs said. 'Me and Dirk learned today that he used to be a Pinkerton man. Farley come back from Alder. He remembered seeing him there.'

'If he was a Pinkerton man, then he likely

still is,' Reardon murmured. 'So that's what he and Larabee had to talk about.' He drove his fist into his palm. 'All the more reason we have to get moving. Between Larabee, Peters and the weather, we can't take any chances. And Larabee knows something. He deliberately beat Kessler badly—to put him out of action.'

He took a turn around the room. 'All right, finish your drink and get out of here. I've got some thinking to do. See Kessler in the morning, and as soon as you know, tell me when he can ride.'

When Briggs had gone, Reardon dropped into a chair and lit a cigar. He smoked slowly, his eyes staring out at nothing while he assessed the events of the last days. The more he considered all that had happened since Larabee's arrival, the more convinced he was that Larabee and Peters were working together. And now little things about Larabee began to make sense: some of his unconscious movements, his way of saying things.

'An Army man, I'll stake my life on it!' Reardon said aloud.

He returned to his thinking. Then he rose. He would go to the hotel and see if Larabee was still awake. It would be natural enough for him to congratulate Larabee. And from there, he could ask a few questions that just might tell him a little more of what Larabee knew.

Reardon was passing the mouth of the alley separating the rear of the hotel from the small stable when he heard the clop of hooves. He moved forward, staying in shadow, but positioning himself so that he could see what was happening. He watched as Larabee on his chestnut rode under the night light above the stable door and started up the alley.

Reardon waited until Larabee was out of sight. Then he hurried back to his house, where he saddled his black. Getting his guns, he buckled them on, mounted, and started east, making a swing through the hills and coming down into the chopped up country by a back trail. He could see Larabee well ahead, outlined by the freshly risen late moon. He was not surprised when he saw another rider come out of shadow and ride alongside the chestnut. Peters, he guessed. And now Reardon knew he had been right in linking the pair together.

*   *   *

Larabee and Peters pushed their horses through the twisting canyons. Peters had brought a pair of bull's-eye lanterns and now and then lit his when the high canyon walls cut away the light of the late moon. Neither spoke except when necessary until they reached their destination. Peters grunted in relief when Larabee pulled up in a patch of bright moonlight.

'I thought you were going to ride us into the river.'

Larabee stepped out of the saddle. 'You've been this far before?'

'Twice,' Peters admitted. 'But like all the Army men, it never occurred to me anyone could get a train of loaded mules up into that cut.'

'Half of my finding it was lucky,' Larabee said. 'All right, bring your lantern and let's get at it.'

He found the moonlight sufficient to guide him up the face of the rock. A moment later Peters joined him and they moved into the deep-walled cut where they needed the bull's-eyes. Peters flashed his half jokingly into Larabee's face.

'It doesn't look like Kessler landed very many on you.'

'One,' Larabee confessed. 'And it was almost the end of things. As it is, he won't be around to bother us for a few days.' He reached the Z bend and stopped, shining his lantern under the overhang where the stack of planks and coils of rope were hidden. Peters swore in surprise.

'Someone did a lot of thinking and planning,' he said. 'And someone else did a lot of work. To get all those mules up here was no one or two man job.'

'I still like Kessler and his crew,' Larabee said. 'In my book, they fit the picture.'

'I'd agree if the Army men hadn't searched their camp twice,' Peters said. 'And the time

Reardon grubstaked Kessler for that month, he was up there too. He said there wasn't even a whiff of mule—and he had a look in all the tunnels around the camp.'

'Whoever was smart enough to fool everyone by ramping the mules up to this cut would be smart enough to hide them safely in the mountains,' Larabee pointed out.

'Someone like . . . Lynn?'

'I didn't say that,' Larabee retorted. 'All right, let's get started.'

They worked as quickly as the awkward weight and length of the planks permitted. The chill of late night deepened but neither man noticed as long as he was moving. Once, when they were rigging the slanting ramp of planking from the mouth of the cut down to the trail, clouds scudded over the moon, slowing their work. But finally the job was done—the planks slanting upward along the rock wall of the canyon and anchored to outcroppings by the ropes. At the sides of the mouth of the cut, Larabee located the holes that had been drilled in the rock to hold the metal pins. Once he had the pins driven into place and the ropes threaded through their eyelets, the job was finished. Peters was at the bottom of the plank ramp, and Larabee walked heavily down to meet him. The planking swayed but held steady.

'It'll support a horse and rider easily enough,' he said.

Peters' answer was to climb aboard his horse and ride it up the planking and into the cut. Here he dismounted and looked down at Larabee.

'No trouble,' Peters said. He studied the drop to the canyon floor. 'I can get him down by making him jump at an angle. Maybe we'd be smart to take the planks away now—just in case some snoop comes along.'

'It's too high to risk it,' Larabee said. 'We'll take a chance on anyone snooping. I want you back in town in one piece—and as soon as you see or hear or smell anything suspicious.' His voice had the crack of a Cavalry officer's in it. 'So don't try to play the hero, Dan. You've made up for any earlier mistakes. Remember that.'

'Yes, sir,' Peters said mockingly. He saluted Larabee and swung his paint around. 'I'll see you in the mountains, if you can find your way along the top of this canyon.'

'If' was a good word, Larabee thought. According to Peters and to the Army reports he had read, no one had managed to trace the end of any of the major canyons from up above—mainly, he guessed, because they became too narrow and were dug too deeply to be seen from the top except by sheer luck.

Still, it was his job to try again. And he reined the chestnut around, heading it back the way they had come.

*   *   *

Brooks Reardon lay belly-down on top of a ridge that gave a narrow view of the brawling creek and the canyon that ran into it. From his vantage point he could focus his field glasses well enough to just barely make out what Larabee and Peters were doing at the mouth of the cut. Reardon swore softly. Peters was no fool. As soon as he reached the distant end of the cut, he would know where the mules were and how they'd been hidden from the Army.

And then what? Reardon wondered. Then he or Larabee would report to the nearest Army post, and there would be no chance of getting the ammunition to the central cache. All trails would be blocked off. Reardon swore again, louder this time. Without that ammunition, half the guns he had hidden would be useless. Without it, he knew he couldn't realize enough money to do more than pay off Kessler and his men, let alone make the profit he needed so desperately for himself.

His first thought was to go after Larabee, to stop him in case he should be heading right now to report to the Army. Mounting his black, he rode down from the ridge and took a twisting trail that brought him out on another high point. From here he could see the land above the canyons, still washed by moonlight and, now, by the breaking dawn.

Reardon laughed suddenly. Larabee wasn't heading for any Army post. The fool was riding south. He was obviously trying to find an overland route to the end of the cut! Well let him hunt. He'd play the devil just keeping from getting himself lost.

Once more Reardon dropped downslope. He reached the trail leading to town but turned east to drop into the canyon. He made the turn southward with the ease of one who knows the country well and let the black move at a leisurely pace. There was no need to hurry now. Peters had no way out except by this trail. All Reardon had to do was wait for him to show up.

Reining in, Reardon checked his guns and then rode on again.

CHAPTER EIGHT

Full daylight showed clear and blue above Peters as he reached the end of the cut. He patted the paint as he slipped from the saddle. Since leaving the mouth of the cut, the trail had sloped slowly but steadily uphill, and the horse was obviously tired. While he was climbing, Peters noticed that the canyon walls kept deepening. Now he had to crane his neck far back to see the distant rim of the rock walls that enclosed him on three sides.

Peters walked around slowly, his eyes studying the canyon floor. The sun seldom penetrated here for long and the late spring and the summer rains had washed away a good deal of the sign he had seen earlier. Even so, he could make out enough prints to know that the mule train had been led this far.

He knew where he was because by backing away from the end wall of the canyon, he could see the three jagged fingers of Old Sawtooth, the mountain that fed the creek where Kessler's 'miners' had their camp. Just south and west of where he stood must be the miners' camp, he thought.

'With about a quarter mile of rock between them and us,' he told the paint.

Hungry, he took some prepared food from his saddlebags and spent a little time eating.

He washed it down with careful gulps of water from his canteen. Then he poured a little water into the lid of the ancient Army messkit he carried and let the paint have a drink. That done, he lit a cigar and studied the apparently solid rock walls, trying to imagine how the mules could have reached this point and then disappeared so completely.

He was leaning against the east wall, taking the final puffs on his stogie when the early sun slanted down and sprayed the west wall with its thin golden light. Suddenly he could see that the wall wasn't nearly as solid as it looked. He walked quickly to it and stared at what clearly was loosely stacked rock rising a good thirty feet and then blending into the smoother, more solid face of the cliff.

Stepping back, Peters took a few quick steps and leaped lightly up to what he had first thought a narrow ledge of rock. He swore as it shook under his weight. Then it settled back and he stared down thoughtfully. Finding a more solid place to put one foot and a small outcropping for his grip, he began to thrust his weight against the loose rock. He thrust harder as he felt it slide. Then he whooped with pleasure as it gave a grumble of protest and tumbled free to roll out into the trail.

Now Peters had to use his solid foot- and handholds to pull himself free as rocks that the loose boulder had been supporting began to shift. He clung to the cliff face and watched a miniature slide develop as rock after rock dropped away from the wall and piled up below. Finally the slide stopped. The dust settled on the still morning air.

Gingerly, Peters lowered himself back to the ground and stared at the hole he had uncovered. If the rubble was cleared from the bottom of the hole, Peters thought, he would have a tunnel a good ten feet high and half again as wide. Whistling softly to himself, he got his bull's-eye lantern and carefully climbed over the rubble until he was well inside the hole. The feeble light from the lantern was quickly swallowed by darkness that stretched ahead of him, but there was glow enough for him to see the smooth rock floor beyond where he stood.

But his nose told him more than his eyes could. A faint drift of air moved around his head, coming from the direction he faced, and on that air was the strong aroma of stable, the unmistakable odor of mules and horses kept confined in a small space.

Peters scrambled back to the paint, put away the lantern, and climbed into the saddle. 'That's all we need,' he said cheerfully. 'I don't know where the other end of that tunnel is, but I'll bet my law books that an Army detachment can find it, now that they know what to look for.' Slapping the paint lightly, he started it back down the trail.

He felt at peace with his conscience for the

first time in quite a while. It had taken Larabee's sharp eye and maybe a bit of luck to find the key to the puzzle. But he had done his share too now. Almost, he corrected himself. There was still the nagging worry about Lynn's possible part in this.

The devil with it, he decided. He would return to town and talk to her, tell her what he had been doing, and what he'd found. He was sure that he knew her well enough to be able to know what her expression would mean. And deep inside, he was hoping that Larabee's guess had been no more than that—a guess; that Lynn was no more than what she seemed to be—a handsome woman with a flair for business and with the determination to be a success. 'But honestly,' he told the paint, 'it's hard to think of Lynn any other way, isn't it, boy?'

The paint lifted its ears as if in agreement. Peters rode on, feeling somewhat better. He was whistling as he reached the drop-off and reined the paint in. He dismounted, took the reins, and led the paint carefully down the swaying, sloping planking. He grunted in relief as he stepped to the dirt floor of the canyon and drew the paint after him. Mounting, he started for the sharp bend a short distance ahead. He reined in, frowning as he heard the quick beat of hooves from that direction.

Larabee? He shook his head and reached for his gun. Larabee would be up above, trying to trace the canyon from the top. Before he could get his gun free, a rider on a black horse swept around the bend and into plain sight.

Peters let his hand fall away from his gun butt. 'Brooks!' he shouted. He pointed behind him. 'I just found out how the raiders got the mules away. I—'

He stopped, the excitement draining out of him. He stared at the carbine Reardon carried across his saddle bow, the muzzle aimed forward, aimed at him. Understanding was like a dousing of icy water.

'You!' Peters whispered.

Reardon was less than a dozen feet away now. He reined up, the gun muzzle holding steadily on its target. 'Me,' he agreed. 'Sorry, Dan.'

'You and Kessler?' Reardon nodded. Peters went on, 'Why, damn it? With everything you've got, everything you have to look forward to . . .'

'Everything I've got!' Reardon repeated. He laughed. 'Do you know what I have, Dan? Debts! My store mortgaged, my share of the hotel borrowed on, my bank in trouble.' He stopped laughing and swore viciously. 'If that fool railroad hadn't postponed its plans to build through Montana, I'd be a rich man now. As it is, I'll be out of debt by spring and comfortable enough until the railroad starts building and makes me rich.'

'No,' Peters said. 'Before spring you'll be

hanging at the end of an Army rope.'

Reardon shook his head and gave his soft chuckle. 'Not a chance, Dan. Because nobody except Kessler and his crew knows that I'm behind the raids. And they aren't about to give me away,' he finished mockingly.

'I know,' Peters said. 'Larabee will know before long.'

'Larabee is crawling all over the hills trying to find something he'll never see,' Reardon answered.

Peters stared at the unwavering muzzle of the carbine. 'Larabee was,' he agreed. 'But take a look at the sun. It's reaching for midmorning, for the time when he and I are supposed to meet.'

'I'll take that chance,' Reardon answered. But seemingly unable to help himself, he half turned in the saddle as if to look back over his shoulder.

Peters went for the gun at his hip. He was no expert but he could draw with respectable speed. He felt the butt of the gun slap against his palm, felt the muzzle clear leather. And then he felt the impact of Reardon's carbine slug as it smashed into his unprotected belly.

The paint suddenly seemed to bolt out from under him. The ground rushed up with terrifying speed and struck him viciously. He fought for air and found it—and with it came the first of the pain. He thought, *Dying isn't any pleasure,* and let darkness wipe the pain and shock from his mind.

Reardon slid the carbine back into its boot. 'You can't say I shot an unarmed man,' he observed to his black. With a half choked laugh, he reined around and rode for open country.

The moving sun stroked across Peters' blood-drained face and moved on. Shadows lengthened and coolness moved into the canyon. Finally Peters' eyes opened and he stared at the world he thought he had left for good. He could feel the pain burning deep inside him, and when he touched his middle, his fingers met the sticky warmth of oozing blood.

But he was alive! The thought stirred strength inside him. He looked around and saw the paint, reins dangling, standing not far away. He worked his mouth until he found enough saliva to wet his lips. He whistled and the paint came to him. Grasping a stirrup, he pulled himself slowly, agonizingly to his feet. He stood gasping, seeking the muscle control he needed to crawl into the saddle.

After a time he found it, and he sat for a long time, both hands gripping the horn. When the fog cleared from his mind, he took his rope and lashed himself into the saddle. Every move was slow, as if he were moving under water. But finally the job was done and he could turn the horse and start it for Glory Hole.

As he rode, the pain began to hammer inside him violently. He tried to drown it out, making his mind say over and over, *See McFee and Larabee. Tell Larabee what happened. See McFee and Larabee. Tell . . .*

The last of the sun slanted into his eyes as he came up out of the canyon and started across the flat for Glory Hole. His face was beaded with sweat. It dripped into his eyes and he wiped at it with the back of his hand so that he could see more clearly. But soon wiping did no good. The mist stayed over his eyes, thickening until it finally blotted out all sight.

He rode blind the last long minutes. He was barely aware of the change in sound as the paint left the trail and started down the harder packed dirt of the main street. Vaguely he heard a voice lifted in surprise, heard the hammering of running feet on the board sidewalk, and then heard the voice of Lynn Graham.

'Dan! Dan, what happened?' There was no answer and she said, 'Quick, take him into my rooms. And get Dr. McFee. Hurry, please!'

Peters felt himself lifted, carried. His mind groped for the meaning in this and found no answer. Then he felt the softness of something against his back, the coolness of moisture on his face. Once more he heard Lynn's voice calling his name.

With an effort he forced some of the mists from his mind. Deep down in his brain was something important, something he had to tell her. No, tell Larabee. That was it! He had to warn Larabee about Brooks Reardon.

He heard Lynn talking but her words made no sense. His mind was straining to get his mouth to shape the words. And when she said, 'Dan, who did this? Who shot you? Dan . . .'

And finally his mouth opened. His lips moved. He said thinly but clearly, 'Larabee.' And he thought he said, 'Tell Larabee Brooks shot me. Tell him . . .' But those words were only echoes in his mind.

His head dropped to one side as the mists closed over him again. Lynn straightened up. 'Larabee,' she repeated aloud. The other night he and Dan had fought with words. And today with guns. And now Dan was dying.

Larabee, she thought. Turning away from Peters' still body, she went to her desk and looked at the .38 lying in a drawer. Once the doctor had taken Dan away, she would load the gun. Then she would sit and wait—wait for Larabee's return.

CHAPTER NINE

For Larabee, the day was a long and empty one. With the slanting of the sun, he turned the chestnut toward town. He was on a slope of the foothills, the mountains rising sheer behind him, and he stared down at the sprawl of chopped up land stretching below. He grunted in disgust. Somewhere in that maze was the upper rim of the canyon where he had left Peters. But search as he might, he had been unable to find any trace of it. Larabee suspected that the canyon was one of those cut so deeply that to tell it from above was impossible.

Still, he thought, Peters should have had more success than he. The whole day wouldn't have been wasted. With that thought lifting his spirits, Larabee pushed the chestnut as fast as the rough trail allowed. Even so, full dark had come by the time he reached town. He pushed the chestnut down the alley and reined into the stable behind the hotel. He gave a grunt of satisfaction when he saw Peters' paint in its stall.

The night hostler had come on duty, and Larabee said, 'Rub him down good and see that he gets extra oats. He's had a long day.'

Leaving the man to unsaddle the horse, Larabee went into the hotel by the rear door, passed Lynn Graham's quarters, and walked on into the lobby. He looked around for Peters, first in the dining room and then in the bar. He saw Finley coming from Lynn's quarters and he said, 'I'm looking for Dan Peters.'

The old man nodded, the muscles of his face tightening the wrinkles. His voice was almost curt as he said, 'Miss Graham'd like to see you. On the left.'

'I know,' Larabee said. With a nod of thanks, he went back down the hall and rapped on her door.

Lynn Graham's voice called steadily, 'Come in.'

Larabee lifted the latch and stepped into the room. He stopped abruptly and stared at the gun trained on him. She was sitting on her sofa, facing the door, and holding her .38 steadily. Her expression was strained, her eyes glittering in the lamplight.

'Close the door, please.' There was no emotion in her voice.

Larabee shut the door behind him. He said, 'I'm looking for Dan Peters . . .'

'Why? Were you surprised to find him gone when you went back to where you left him?'

He stared at her, wondering if she had been gripped by some strange madness. 'What the devil are you talking about?' he demanded. 'Where's Peters? And point that gun somewhere else!'

'Dan is dead,' she said in the same empty voice. 'Dr. McFee did all he could but it was too late. He thinks Dan might have lived if he'd had help earlier. But he bled to death— inside.'

Larabee thought, *Peters let himself get trapped by the raiders. He must have found something and got caught before he could ride away.*

He said, 'I'm sorry,' and realized how foolish his words must sound.

'Sorry that you didn't make sure he was dead before you rode off and left him? Sorry that he had enough spirit to ride all the way here so he could tell me who shot him?'

Larabee stared at her, and now things were becoming clear. He took a slow, steadying breath. 'I left Dan at daylight. He hadn't been shot then. And I didn't go back and shoot him.' He saw no change in the deadly emptiness of her expression. 'Why would I kill him?' Larabee demanded. 'We were working together.'

'Oh? Working at what, Mr. Larabee?'

Her icy calm—the ice so thin and brittle— made him more sure than ever that she was on the edge of madness. He kept his eyes on the gun aimed at him. Working at what? she'd asked. He considered trying to tell her and decided against it. If she was involved in the raids, he couldn't risk letting her know just how much he had found out. And if she wasn't, how much chance was there that she would believe him? He thought sourly that, either way, she was going to find a reason to shoot him.

He said flatly, 'I don't believe that Peters came here and told you I shot him!'

'He rode here dying,' she said. 'He said one word: Larabee! He tried to say more but he was too weak.'

'So he said my name. How do you know he wasn't trying to tell you to find me, to give me a message?'

'I asked him who shot him and he said your name.' Her voice was still empty except for that icy chill. 'Don't you think I've considered all the possibilities, Mr. Larabee? I've been sitting here since they took Dan to the hospital. I've been alone, thinking, except for the minute it took the doctor to come over and tell me that Dan had died.'

Her voice shook a little as if it might break. Now Larabee shifted his gaze to her face. It would be there that he would see the first warning, the shattering of the calm that gripped her; and only when it shattered would she be capable of pulling the trigger of her gun.

She went on, 'I never pictured you as a killer, but then I've never known many killers. I tried to find some other meaning to his word. I couldn't. I can't.'

'He was trying to tell you to find me,'

Larabee said. 'He had something important to tell me. That's the only answer that makes sense: he wanted to tell me what he found and who shot him.'

'And what did he find, or what was he supposed to find?'

'I'm sorry. I can't tell you that.' He tried to ease the tension a little. 'Perhaps we should see McFee, in case Dan said something before he died.'

'He didn't regain consciousness,' she said. 'I want an answer to my question, Mr. Larabee. I want to know what Dan was doing that cost him his life!'

'While you're asking questions, you might try asking why I should shoot him.'

'Everyone in town knows that you and he had words the other night. That he was furious with you.' She moved her head from its rigid position, tilting it slightly as he moved a few feet toward her. 'Maybe whatever you fought about meant so much to Dan that he tried to kill you, and you shot him defending yourself. But even if you did, you had no right to leave him like that . . . to bleed to death miles from here!'

Larabee moved again and saw her gun arm stiffen slightly. He changed direction, sliding now toward her desk on his right. 'Dan and I patched up our fight a few hours after we had it. The fault was mine. I admitted as much. But we let people think we were still at odds. We wanted them to stop thinking of us together.'

'Why?'

He was almost to the desk now. He said, 'If I told you, why should you believe me? You've made up your mind. My words won't change it.'

'No,' she agreed. 'Nothing you can say—or do—will change my mind. I have room for only one idea: to make you pay for what you did to Dan.'

Her face crumpled as her iron will broke. He heard her take a deep sobbing breath and he saw the strain ripple across the back of her hand as she tightened her finger on the trigger. He reached behind him and closed his fingers over a small box on the desktop.

He moved, bringing his arm around and throwing the box at her and at the same time diving for the floor. He landed on his shoulder and rolled toward the sofa.

She didn't shoot. The box struck the sofa inches from her side and she drew back as if she'd been scalded. She started to stand, turning to bring the gun to bear on him again. But now it was too late. Larabee was up and reaching for her arm. He gripped it and jerked, sending the gun flying.

'My apologies,' he said thinly. Still gripping her arm, he spun her so that she fell on the sofa. Grabbing up a pillow, he pressed it over her face to prevent her from screaming. Quickly, deftly, he ripped the fringe from the bottom of the sofa and tied her wrists and ankles with it. That done, he took his kerchief and made ready to gag her.

When he lifted the pillow from her face, she said, 'That won't be necessary. I don't intend to cry for help.'

Larabee realized suddenly that she had made no struggle, no attempt to free herself while he was tying her. He said, 'It isn't your right to be judge, jury, and executioner. That's up to a duly constituted legal body.'

'No legal body was engaged to marry Dan,' she said quietly. 'None was in love with him.'

He stared thoughtfully down at her, holding the pillow ready in case she should crack again. But the icy calm had returned to her. He said, 'I can only tell you that I didn't kill Dan. I can't prove it now. Later, perhaps. I can only ask you to believe me.'

'Why should I? What can you tell me later that you can't tell me now? Why can't you?'

'Because,' he said flatly, 'I'm not sure about you.' He bent to put the gag in her mouth. Then he added, 'Let me ask a question. Why didn't you tell anyone Peters said I shot him— or so you understood?'

'How do you know I didn't?' she demanded.

Larabee said, 'Because if you had I would have been arrested the minute I rode into town. The marshal would have been waiting, or there would have been a mob with a rope. But I don't believe you told even old Finley.

95

He's upset about Dan, I suppose—but there was no hate in him when he talked to me.'

'I didn't tell anyone because I want to kill you myself,' she said coldly. 'And I won't muff the next chance. You can run now, but you can't run forever, Mr. Larabee. Sooner or later I'll find you. And when I do, I won't let you trick me. I'll kill you.'

Larabee waited until she finished and opened her lips to take a breath. Then he deftly slipped the kerchief into her mouth and tied it with the last piece of sofa fringe. He tested the cords around her wrists and ankles, decided they were strong enough, and turned away.

Leaving her, he locked the door and turned to her desk. He disliked what he had to do now and so he did it as quickly as possible. He went through her papers, returning them carefully to their pigeonholes and drawers. Then with a muttered apology, he went into her bedroom and searched there. Finally he returned to the parlor.

There was nothing that indicated any connection between Lynn Graham and the raiders, no single scrap of paper that he could even imagine had any meaning along that line. He knew that a lack of evidence proved nothing in a case of this kind; she was a clever woman, possibly too clever to leave any damning papers around. Still, it was a small point in her favor.

He went to the door. 'Someone will come along soon to free you.' With a nod, he unlocked the door and went out. He used the key to lock it from the outside and took the key with him. Now he moved quickly, going upstairs for his gear and hurrying out to the stable. He saddled the chestnut under the startled gaze of the hostler, tied his gear behind the saddle, mounted, and rode down the alley.

At the livery, he rented a pack horse, bought a pack saddle and a bag of oats, and rode back up the dark alley to the rear of the mercantile. He could see a crack of light coming from somewhere inside and he used his gun butt to hammer loudly on the door. Finally a tired-eyed man pulled it open.

'The store's shut for the night . . .'

'Fine,' Larabee said. 'Then I won't have to wait to get served.' He showed the man his gun. 'Let's do some marketing.'

'I'm just the bookkeeper. I don't—'

'You can keep tally on what I pick out. I figure on paying,' Larabee said. He let himself in. 'Now move. And bring a lamp.'

Larabee needed little time to decide what to choose. Too often he had had to take to the trail for an indefinite length of time. Now with the quickness of long practice he had a sack loaded with bacon and beans, flour, some fresh meat, tobacco for his pipe, coffee, a block of tea and one of chocolate. That, along with the things he carried in his saddlebags, should see him through, he decided.

He paid the bookkeeper and then gave him extra money. 'That's for Miss Graham, to pay my hotel bill,' he said. With a nod, he went out, loaded his sack on the pack horse, mounted the chestnut, and started out of the alley. At its mouth, he turned south into the hills behind town, and then swung east. Once over the rise and into the chopped up land, he put his heels into the chestnut's flanks, sending it hurtling through the darkness with the pack animal galloping awkwardly behind.

CHAPTER TEN

Reardon spent the afternoon working in his bank, trying to hide his impatience as the hours dragged slowly on. It took all his will to keep himself under control until it was late enough for him to go to the Cattleman's and signal Briggs.

When evening finally came, he drifted down to the saloon. He ordered his drink and glanced around casually. Only half a dozen customers were in sight, and none was Briggs. Pushing down a desire to swear, Reardon picked up his drink and nodded to the bartender. 'Quiet in here since that Kessler landed in the hospital. Even his sidekick—what's his name?—doesn't seem to be around.'

'Briggs,' the bartender said. 'I ain't seen him since he helped haul Kessler over to the doc's place.'

Reardon finished his drink and went up the street to the hotel. The saloon bar here was empty except for the man behind the bar. Reardon ordered whiskey. The bartender poured it, saying, 'Hell of a thing about Mr. Peters, wasn't it?'

Reardon's hand reaching for the glass stopped with a jerk. 'Peters?' He felt the sudden hammering of his heart and pulled his hand back to keep the bartender from seeing its shaking. 'What about him?'

'He was shot today. Back in the hills someplace, I guess. But he rode all the way to town. And with a bullet in his belly too.'

Came to town—alive! Reardon made himself hold his hand steady enough to lift the glass and down his whiskey. He managed to say, 'Nobody said anything about it. When—when did he show up?'

'About sundown. I guess most folks haven't heard yet. There wasn't anybody around but me and Finley. We caught him when he was falling off his horse. Miss Graham had us pack him to her rooms and then go for the doc.'

Reardon took a deep, steadying breath. 'He's still alive?' he heard himself ask.

'I haven't heard. But he was breathing when we took him to Miss Graham's parlor. He was out cold, but still alive.'

Reardon said, 'What about the marshal? Has he seen Dan yet?'

'He's been gone all day. Off to Alder for something or other.'

Reardon waved aside the offer of another drink and hurried out to where Finley sat behind the hotel desk. He said, 'I just heard about Dan Peters. Is Miss Graham all right?'

'I ain't seen her since she called me in and told me to have Larabee see her as soon as he come in.'

'When was that?'

'Quite a time after the doc took Peters

away,' Finley said. 'He's a nice fellow. I hope he'll be all right.'

'Everybody likes Dan,' Reardon said, and turned away. He moved down the hall slowly. His mind shouted at him, *Larabee!* After McFee had taken Peters away, Lynn had asked for Larabee to come to her. That could only mean that Peters had regained consciousness and talked, that he had told her what had happened and had asked her to get his message to Larabee as quickly as possible.

He stopped. No, if that was true, why hadn't he been arrested before now? Then he remembered that the marshal was away. He remained standing, turning and twisting what little he knew, trying to decide just how much Lynn had been told by Peters. He thought, *If Dan had told her I shot him, she would have come gunning for me.* Because that was the kind of woman Lynn Graham struck him as: self-sufficient, ready and able to do her own work when she had to.

There was only one way to find out, Reardon knew. Taking a deep breath, he walked to Lynn's door and knocked. He heard no sound from inside. Frowning, he tried the latch. The door was locked. *The devil,* he thought. Where had she gone—to the hospital or hunting him? She and Larabee!

He was about to turn away when he heard a heavy thudding sound from inside. He rapped on the door again. 'Lynn?' The sound was repeated. Reardon used his passkey to open the door. He gasped in surprise at the sight of Lynn Graham, turkey trussed, lying on the floor and throwing her body up so that it would thump as she slammed down.

He freed her with a few slashes of his pocketknife. Helping her to the sofa, he stared at her, seeking some clue in her expression. 'What happened here?'

She tried to speak and failed. Reardon rose and got her a glass of water. She gulped it down and then managed to squeeze words out. 'Larabee,' she said. 'He tied me up and rode away. He—he shot Dan! He killed the man I was going to marry!'

For the first time her self-possession left her completely. She lowered her head and began to sob softly. Reardon put an arm awkwardly around her shoulders, glad that she couldn't see the relief that must be showing on his face. Larabee! She thought Larabee had killed Peters.

He listened while she described what had happened from the time of Peters' arrival until Larabee had gone. Reardon couldn't understand why Larabee had refused to tell Lynn what he and Peters had been doing, but he could see the value of Larabee's silence to him. Because Larabee must know a lot about the cache of ammunition. He must have had a good idea where to look even if Peters hadn't had a chance to talk to him. That meant he had to find out where Larabee was heading: for the Army post or to find the cache himself. And either way he had to stop Larabee as soon as possible.

He said, 'Did Larabee say where he was going?'

'No.' She lifted her head and looked into Reardon's face. 'He's been gone over half an hour. You'd never catch up with him.'

'I can try,' he said. 'Remember, Kessler and Briggs followed him around for a time—or so Larabee claimed. They just might know what part of the country interested Larabee the most. And he might head back that way.'

'But he just rode around looking at Lazy B land,' she said.

Before he could stop himself, Reardon said, 'I heard he spent quite a lot of time up in the hills too, near old Sawtooth.' He stood up quickly, not wanting to risk saying any more. 'If you're all right, I'll go talk to Kessler and see if he knows anything that might help.'

'I'm fine now. Thank you, Brooks.' Her voice was thin and strained and she looked away from him.

Reardon hurried out and started down the alley for McFee's hospital. He met the doctor at the door. 'I want to talk to Kessler. I just found Lynn roped like a steer. She said Larabee did it, that Dan claimed Larabee shot him. Kessler might know . . .'

McFee snorted. 'Larabee? That doesn't

103

make sense. Before he died, Peters told me he had an important message for Larabee and I was to get it to him. He was trying to get the words out when he died.' He pushed out his lip. 'He sounded eager to talk to Larabee, not mad at him.'

'Maybe he was out of his head,' Reardon said weakly. 'Did he say who did shoot him if it wasn't Larabee?'

'No. He wasn't conscious longer'n enough to tell me what I just told you.' McFee swore softly. 'And he was a little fevered because the animal that did shoot him left him with a bullet in his belly and not dead—left him to die in the middle of nowhere about as painful a way as a man can die. But he was clear-headed enough when he talked to me.'

'Then what is Larabee running from?' Reardon demanded. He added, 'Let me talk to Kessler, maybe he—'

'Kessler packed himself out of here about twenty minutes back. Briggs come riding in and bulled right to his bed. Whatever he said made Kessler climb out of bed, bruises and all.'

Reardon nodded and turned away. He returned to the stable and hurried up to the smelly room Briggs and Kessler used. He found both men there, readying themselves for the trail.

Kessler said, 'Where the devil you been? Briggs looked all over for you. That Larabee must have figured out something from Peters getting shot. Briggs was east of the saddle and he says he saw Larabee riding like the devil was after him and towing a pack horse. And it looks like he's heading for our camp.'

'I suspect he is,' Reardon said. 'All right, you two go after him. No, wait. Take the cutoff and get to the camp as fast as you can. Load the mules and start them moving down the trail. I'll follow behind Larabee and make sure he doesn't get too close.'

Kessler showed his missing tooth in a grin. 'The way you took care of Peters, maybe?'

'Forget Peters.' He started away.

Briggs said, 'That Graham woman took off east on her sorrel just as me and Dirk was coming into the alley. We figure maybe she's working with Larabee and gone to help him.'

'I'll see about it,' Reardon said. Chuckling as he realized now the meaning of the strange thinness in Lynn's voice, he hurried away to saddle his horse. Just as he had feared she would come gunning for him if she thought he'd shot Dan Peters, so now she was out to kill Larabee. She had admitted trying to shoot him before and failing. But he doubted if she'd fail given a second chance. He laughed aloud as he put his black on the trail.

*　　　*　　　*

Lynn, dressed in her riding clothes, gun belted

around her waist, pushed her leggy sorrel mare up the slope toward the Lazy B. Her mind was so consumed with the desire to find Larabee, to make him pay for shooting Dan Peters, that she was unaware of the horse and rider following at a discreet distance. She pulled into the rear yard of the ranch and dropped to the ground, hurrying toward the lighted kitchen. Just as she entered the house, Reardon swung his black into shadow alongside the barn.

He was debating whether to risk slipping up to the kitchen window in an effort to hear what she and Barling might be saying when the door opened and Lynn came out, Barling behind her. They walked directly toward the barn, talking as they came.

'I still can't picture that Larabee fellow as the kind who'd kill a man like Dan Peters,' Barling was saying.

'Your opinion doesn't mean anything to me,' she said with unusual tartness. 'Dan as good as said that Larabee killed him. Now will you please hurry and get my supplies and pack horse ready?'

'The boys are putting your gear together,' he said stiffly. 'I'll get old Graybeard out right now. He's the best pack horse we got. He's surefooted—and that sorrel better be too if you figure on riding the trails around old Sawtooth the way you said you were.'

'I intend to do just that,' she said. They disappeared into the barn. Moments later they reappeared, Barling leading a big gray horse with a pack saddle snug on its back. Reardon remained where he was, watching as two cowhands came from the house and loaded camping gear and food on the gray. Lynn nodded her thanks and climbed aboard her sorrel.

'If you won't stay until morning, at least let me send one of the boys along,' Barling worried.

'This is my affair and I'll handle it alone, thank you.' She added a bit less tartly, 'If I'd wanted a posse, Mr. Barling, I'd have rounded one up in town. As for my staying until morning, since you admit having given Larabee help less than an hour ago, I can hardly waste the time sleeping here.'

Reardon whistled silently as she rode off, leading the gray. So Larabee had stopped here, and Barling had helped him. How? Reardon answered his own question quickly enough. Barling knew these nearby mountains as well as any man in these parts. He could have told Larabee about the location of many possible hideouts. He might even know about the tunnel that ran through the canyon to the miners' camp—or that had until Kessler's boys had cleverly filled in the canyon end.

Reardon decided that if he kept fairly close behind Lynn, sooner or later she would lead him to Larabee. Then, if she didn't kill the man, Reardon decided he would have to. After

107

CHAPTER ELEVEN

When Larabee left Barling, he finally had a destination in mind. But the information had cost him the secrecy of his true identity, and he only hoped what he'd had to say wouldn't backfire on him. But Barling had seemed impressed by Larabee's sweat-stained credentials and he swore he wouldn't tell anyone what he'd just learned.

Once their relationship was established, Larabee settled back in Barling's parlor with coffee and a cigar and outlined to the old man everything that had happened to the present. He left out only his suspicion of Lynn Graham.

After hearing Larabee out, Barling nodded. 'I know that old cut Dan Peters rode up. Until two years ago a ledge sloped up from the lower canyon so a man could ride from one to the other. But a spring flood washed it out. Since then I haven't been in, but I used to have to hunt for stray critters there every once in a while. There used to be a big-mouthed tunnel at the other end. Scary kind of place. It ran all the way through the ridge of rock that makes the west wall of the cut. It came out in a hollow near the base of old Sawtooth.'

He gulped at his coffee. 'But the flood that spring was bad and I expect the mouth of the tunnel got washed shut.'

'A tunnel,' Larabee echoed. 'A tunnel big enough to drive a mule through—a loaded one?'

'Loaded and with a man sitting on top and two side by side,' Barling agreed. His rheumy eyes widened. 'If you're thinking what I figure . . . you just might be right. Them raiders could have run the mules to the end of the cut and then into the tunnel, if they found a way to open it up.'

'Anything a flood washed in could be cleared out with some blasting powder and a crew with picks and shovels,' Larabee said. 'Like a crew of miners.'

Barling slapped a hand down on his knee. 'The hill where that tunnel comes out by old Sawtooth ain't but just over the rise from Kessler's mining camp!'

Larabee said, 'The Army scouted that territory pretty thoroughly. But if they didn't know about the tunnel, they could have been hoodwinked.'

At least, he decided, it was the first real goal he'd had yet. Getting a rough sketch-map from Barling, he thanked the old man and went to his waiting horses. Barling came along, tossing out words of caution.

'The map ain't too clear, but just remember, there's lots of dead end canyons in that country around Sawtooth. If you got to keep going west, you stick to the old prospectors' trail that kinks along the base of the mountain from the north side around to the west slope. From there it goes about as due west as any trail can in these mountains. It climbs right up over a pass in the Bitterroots and drops down into Idaho Territory. It ain't a trail that's been used too much since the gold strike petered out here, but I reckon it'll still take a string of mules and men going single file.'

Larabee said, 'I know the country on the other side of the pass. I've had my share of chousing critters in that country—men, mostly.' He mounted the chestnut, gave his thanks again, and rode off.

He found the trail leading toward the mining camp where Barling said it would be, not too far up behind his big barn. This was the main trail used for driving Lazy B stock in and out of the summer meadows, so it was well trampled and easy riding.

The moon was coming up a bit earlier now, and after a time Larabee could see well enough to risk pushing the horses at a good clip. He reached the first of the high meadows and paused, debating whether to stop and make camp here or push on a ways. He could feel the chill of this higher country, but he decided to push on anyway, and so he crossed the meadow and continued along the trail. It was narrower now, in one place switching back and forth to climb a steep slope.

Here and there thick timber lined the trail, cutting the moonlight to the barest thin filtering of silver. Larabee could feel both horses beginning to tire badly as he topped the rise and rode into a smaller meadow. Here the air was icily cold, with frost forming already on the meadow grass.

Larabee saw the sparkle of a small stream and he turned, following its current along the edge of the meadow to its start in a small pond. Another stream fed the pond and he went along this until he reached a rise of rocks that promised some shelter. He moved into the rocks far enough from the stream so that its steady murmur wouldn't drown any sounds he might care to hear.

He made a quick camp, not bothering with a fire, but eating a cold meal and chasing it down with stream water. With the horses unsaddled, watered, fed and hobbled in a small grassy hollow, Larabee rolled into his blankets, put his back to a rock wall, and went to sleep.

The years of training had made him a light, almost alert sleeper. When the jangle of harness came from the far side of the small meadow, Larabee was instantly awake. He heard the sound again, identified it, and rolled quickly to his feet. Slipping into his boots, he grabbed his greatcoat and worked it on as he trotted back to the edge of the meadow. It was flooded with late moonlight and he could see two horses, the first carrying a slender figure. They moved steadily across the meadow in the direction of old Sawtooth. Even from where he stood, Larabee could recognize Lynn Graham. She rode well, but still she rode woman fashion, and he could think of no other female who would be on this trail tonight, or at any other time.

He grunted, wondering if Barling had told her which way he was heading. As she disappeared into the timber on the far side of the meadow, Larabee turned back toward his camp. Then the pad of another horse flicked across his hearing. He turned and waited. This rider he could not recognize, but he realized that whoever it was had his harness muffled and that he was riding far enough to the rear of Lynn so as not to let her know he was behind her.

Now Larabee hurried back to his camp. He saddled and loaded his horses, wrapped their harness carefully, and then set off after Lynn and the rider following her.

The second rider had disappeared by the time Larabee reached the meadow. Even so, he stayed along the edge, out of the moonlight, until he reached the trail. Then he rode cautiously, peering ahead whenever there was moonlight enough through the trees to let him see. The trail wound back and forth through the heavy timber. Then it began to kink sharply upward, climbing a bare ridge.

Larabee stopped at the edge of the trees and watched as first Lynn Graham and then the other rider worked their way up the slope and out of sight. He was thinking that Lynn couldn't be much of a tracker if she hadn't realized by now that he wasn't ahead of her.

He rode out of the trees and began a slow, steady climb up the barren cliffside. Nearing the top, he stopped his horses, slipped out of the saddle, and eased forward on foot. He could see a bench covered with scattered timber stretching ahead. Beyond it, old Sawtooth rose against the night sky, its snowy slopes glittering in the moonlight. The trail twisted across the bench, angling toward a long outjutting of timbered rock that Larabee remembered from Barling's map. And not far from that shoulder of rock would be the camp of Kessler's miners.

But right now Larabee was more interested in the faint flicker of light that came from the far left side of the bench. Someone—Lynn, he guessed—had set up camp. Either she had grown too tired to ride farther or she had finally realized that Larabee was not ahead of her. But what of the other rider?

Returning to his horses, Larabee rode over the top of the trail and quickly down into the protective shadow of the thin timber. He worked the horses back and forth along the narrow deer tracks until he decided he was too close to Lynn's camp to risk riding any farther. Tying the horses, he angled back toward the trail at a point where there was moonlight enough for him to study the sign. He walked along, stopping now and then to read the story the prints of three horses made. He found the spot where Lynn and her horses had turned to the left. Glancing that way, he saw the flicker of her campfire. He went on. Then the prints of the third horse disappeared, also turning off the trail to the left.

Now Larabee stepped into shadow and began carefully working his way toward Lynn's fire. He drew close enough to hear the murmur of running water, the faint crackle of the fire, the rattle of a cup against a pan. He remained where he was, stilling his own breathing and sorting out the night sounds and those made by Lynn's moving about. Finally he heard what he'd been listening for: the heavy breathing of a horse not far to his right.

Then he pulled quickly behind a tree. The horse was coming his way. Larabee moved swiftly back toward the trail, to a point where he could see the man coming through a patch of moonlight. Larabee stifled a grunt of surprise. Brooks Reardon! What the devil? What was he doing sneaking along behind Lynn Graham?

But Larabee had no time to sort out the answers now. Reardon had reached the trail and was turning west along it, riding toward the outjutting of rock, toward the camp of the miners. As soon as Reardon disappeared, Larabee hurried to his horses. Leaving the bay pack animal, Larabee mounted the chestnut and started after Reardon. When he reached the shoulder of rock, he again left the horse and went forward on foot. The trail went around the base of the rock and then wound down into a wide hollow. Larabee crouched at the top of the drop and watched the dark blotch made by Reardon and his horse. At the far side of the hollow a scatter of faint lights indicated the miners' cabins. As far as Larabee could figure, Reardon had decided that Lynn had lost the trail, and he'd better head for the mule train. He was riding straight for them, openly, making no effort to hide himself.

As he returned to where he had left the pack horse, Larabee began asking himself questions about Brooks Reardon, and he found that he disliked the answers he got. Then he turned his mind to Lynn. As long as she was trailing him, seeking to kill him, he could never finish the job he had come to do. First he had to find the mule train and then when it moved out—as he was sure it would soon—follow it to the central cache. He grimaced. With a woman as dogged as Lynn Graham, he wouldn't have a chance of keeping himself out of sight of a crew as trail-wise as Kessler and his men.

Reaching the pack horse, Larabee tied the chestnut beside it and eased toward Lynn's camp on foot. He stopped at the edge of a small clearing and studied her camp. It was well made, with the fire just large enough for cooking and built in such a position that she could get reflected heat from a smooth-faced rock. It was a neat camp, made by an obviously fairly experienced trailwoman. The only fault he could find was that she had camped too near a running spring. Its sounds, along with those from the fire, were too loud for her to hear a possible pursuer. But then, he thought, maybe she wasn't used to being trailed.

Lynn was still awake, sitting on a log and sipping steaming coffee. A light, damp wind had sprung up and it brought the scent of both her cooking and the coffee to Larabee's nostrils. He felt his empty stomach respond, and he thought too of the warmth of that fire against the pressing chill of this high country.

He studied the layout of her camp. Her horses were off to one side, hobbled where they could graze on frosty grass. Her saddle lay by her bedroll, and he could see the butt of her carbine thrusting up from the boot. She was wearing her thirty-eight.

He thought about waiting until she bedded down and then slipping in to steal her guns. But the odds were too long, and he was too tired to wait that long. He decided instead on a trick he had used before.

Getting the chestnut, he led it as quietly as he could to the edge of the clearing. Lynn still sat on the log, apparently unable to hear the coming of the chestnut above the murmur of water and the crackle of her fire.

Larabee turned the horse, reins wrapped around the horn, aiming its nose toward Lynn's pair of animals. He gave the chestnut a slap on the rump, sending it leaping forward and into the firelight. Lynn leaped up, drawing her gun with a smoothness Larabee had to admire. She had a bead on the chestnut when she seemed to realize that his saddle was empty. Now she started to turn, but she was too late. Larabee was behind her, his hand snaking out and plucking the gun from her fingers. Almost without breaking stride, he crossed to her saddle and pulled out her carbine.

'Sorry to scare you,' he said, 'but I can't afford the time to dodge your bullets. Now if you'll pour me a cup of that fine smelling coffee, we can sit down and talk this over sensibly.'

'I'll see you in Hades before I'll discuss anything with you!' she flared.

Larabee shrugged as if he had expected her reaction and carried the guns to the chestnut. He loosened his rope and appeared to be using it to tie the guns to his saddle. She walked a few steps toward him. 'Do you intend to ride off and leave me alone—unarmed?'

'No,' Larabee said. He swung around suddenly. His rope lifted, made a loop and then, as she turned to dodge, settled neatly over her shoulders. With a quick wrist flip, he drew it taut, pinning her arms to her sides.

'Sorry again,' he said. 'But one way or another you're going to listen to me.' He mounted the chestnut. 'Now let's go for a walk. We'll get my pack horse and then come back and finish that pot of coffee you brewed.'

She merely stood, staring at him with hate-filled eyes.

CHAPTER TWELVE

With his horses hobbled and grazing alongside Lynn's, Larabee poured himself a mug of coffee and lowered himself wearily to a log. Lynn sat nearby, no longer tied but her features still stiff with her anger.

The damp wind was growing stronger. Larabee frowned as he saw it lift a fluff of ash near the fire and ruffle the sheepskin collar turned up around Lynn's face. He said, 'We either move the fire or put a rock windbreak in front of it. Otherwise one of us will wake up with spark burns in the bedding.'

'If you think I'm going to sleep—' she began stiffly.

Larabee gulped hot coffee. 'You'll sleep,' he said. 'You might not be comfortable, but you'll sleep after all the riding you've done.' He waited a moment and then said, 'I told you I had something to say. So listen. It might have some meaning for you.'

'I'm not interested in anything you have to tell me!'

'Not even that Reardon followed you here and then rode on, down to the miners' camp?'

'Brooks? Why should he?'

'Why should I lie about it?' Larabee demanded. Briefly, he told her how he had followed them both from the meadow below.

He spoke softly, evenly, and slowly he could see doubt forming on her features.

Finally she said, 'But why would Brooks follow me that way?'

'As soon as I've packed you back where you belong tomorrow, I aim to find out.'

Her indignation rose again. 'You're packing me nowhere, Mr. Larabee! I took this trail for one reason: to find you and kill you. I don't intend to give up until I've finished my job!'

'You won't have much choice after I rope you in the saddle and head your horses back to Barling's place,' Larabee said. 'By the time you could get untied, get more guns, and get back to where we are now, I expect to be a long ways away.'

He yawned. 'Anyway, for tonight, let's stop arguing. Give me your word that you won't kill me and we can both get a comfortable night's sleep.'

Her hesitation before she snapped 'Yes' told him more plainly than any words exactly what she had in mind. Sighing, he got up and strolled to where his saddle lay on the ground. Bending, he unrolled his bedding. With his body blocking her view of his hands, he untied his rope. When he turned, he pulled the same trick on her as he had before. But this time she almost got free, realizing only seconds too late what he had in mind.

As the rope settled over her and pinned her arms, she cried, 'I gave you my word!'

Larabee said dryly, 'A lady once told me that a woman has to use every weapon she can to make her way in a man's world, and that saying one thing to a man and doing another thing was about the best of her weapons. You know as well as I that you didn't figure on keeping your promise.'

She refused to answer, merely glaring at him. Larabee wrapped a few loops of rope about her and propelled her to her bedding. He eased her down gently and pulled off her boots. He threw a loop about her ankles and freed her arms. 'Get out of your greatcoat.'

She did so, still stiffly silent. Larabee tied her hands and then ran a line from her wrists to her ankles. Lifting her, he worked her down into her ready-made bedroll.

'You'll be comfortable enough if you don't try to tug free. That will tighten the knots,' he said.

Leaving her fuming, he moved away to build a windbreak before the small fire. That done, he finished the last of the coffee and ate some cold biscuits from his own supplies, smoked a last cigar, and contemplated Lynn's angry face.

At first, she continued to stare at him. But finally weariness and warmth from her bedroll and the fire relaxed her and her eyelids drooped. When her even breathing told him she was asleep, he rose and prepared himself for bed.

Her guns tucked alongside him, Larabee

dropped quickly into his usual light sleep. Daylight and the feel of cold dampness wakened him. He sat up, eyes wide open as he stared at the thick heavy snowflakes spiraling down into his face. His blankets were covered with a good six inches of wet snow. He glanced around. Lynn was barely visible as a motionless mound of white. The coals of the fire were hissing and smoking. The pack saddles with their provisions were almost invisible.

Larabee swore silently and fervently. Of all the things he didn't want, snow came first on his list. And from the way the sky sat down almost on top of them, they could be in for a long, heavy fall. The wind had dropped and the snow sifted straight down in large, damp flakes that he judged were piling up about an inch an hour.

Larabee rose, located his boots under his blankets and pulled them on. He set about reshaping the camp to make it livable. By the time he heard Lynn stirring, he had the fire built up under a slanting shelter of damp pine boughs and he had breakfast cooking. In going through her gear to see if she had clothing suitable for the weather he'd found a small tent. This he put up directly behind where she lay sleeping. He moved her pack of clothing into it and then wakened her.

Untying her ankles and wrists, he nodded at the tent. 'There's dry clothing in there, and

I've heated enough water to give you some for washing up.'

She stared uncomprehendingly at the snow for a moment. Then, without speaking, she went into the tent and drew the flap shut. She came out in a fresh shirt, poured herself some warm water and returned to the tent. When she appeared again, she was washed and her hair was pulled back into a knot at the nape of her neck. She shrugged into a loose, hooded oilskin that fit over her greatcoat, and came to the fire.

She smiled almost wickedly at Larabee. 'Do you play chess, Mr. Larabee?'

'I have.'

'Then you must have figured out by now that you're checkmated. By Mother Nature, too. Or do you imagine you can find a way to send me, roped to the saddle, back down those steep trails alone?'

'No,' Larabee admitted, 'I can't do that. Not now. I've got you on my hands whether I like it or not.'

He dished up bacon and fresh stick bread and handed her a plate. When they were eating, he said, 'The only way we can go is forward. But you might not like what you see when we get over the next rise.' His eyes measured her. 'On the other hand, you might be hoping that there'll be someone there you want to see . . . some of your friends.'

'Just what is that supposed to mean?' she

demanded tartly.

'It'll explain itself later,' he answered. Wiping his plate with stick bread to get the last of the warmth-giving bacon grease, he chewed slowly. 'An October storm like this can go on for a long time or it can break in a hurry and a chinook can come in.'

'At this altitude a chinook wouldn't be of much use,' she said.

'Maybe if we go on, the trail will drop us downslope.' He watched her carefully as he spoke.

She frowned at him. 'Are you trying to say that you don't know where the trail leads but that I might?'

'I wish I knew the answer to that,' he said with flat honesty. Finishing his coffee, he rose and began to break camp.

Wordlessly, she pitched in and helped. He stopped now and then to notice how competently she handled herself even in this kind of weather. She packed most of her own gear, saddled her own horses. Her father had obviously taught her something besides hotel-keeping.

The snow had thinned by the time they were ready for the trail, and Larabee was grateful that they could see a fair distance ahead. Even so, the smaller, harder flakes that fell now were coming in on a thin wind and battering at their faces as they rode.

'North wind,' Larabee said. 'It'll get cold if

it clears off.'

She gave no answer and he rode on, leading the way. After a time he let her take the sorrel and break trail; later, when the chestnut was rested, he took up the chore again. Finally they reached the rise Larabee had climbed last night and for a time they were protected by the outjutting of rock.

'The miners' camp is in a hollow not far ahead,' Larabee said.

'Unless Barling gave us different maps, it should be,' she said dryly.

He gave her a startled glance. 'Then Barling told you he'd seen me and given me a map?' She nodded. He asked, 'What else did he tell you about me?'

'Nothing except that he thought I was wrong, that he didn't believe you could have killed Dan.'

'He knows I didn't,' Larabee said. 'And he knows why.'

'Then why didn't he tell me?' she demanded. There was no belief in her voice.

'Because I swore him to secrecy,' Larabee said. 'Let's rein in here. I'll go to the top of the ridge on foot and take a squint.'

Leaving the chestnut, he got a pair of field glasses from his saddlebags and carried his handgun. 'Are you looking for someone else to shoot now?' she asked tartly.

'They could have a lookout posted,' Larabee said.

'A lookout in this weather? Why should a group of miners post a lookout?'

He studied her. She had sounded sincerely puzzled. He said, 'Since Reardon rode to their camp last night, I assume he warned them that I was on my way. That's reason enough for them to be skittish.'

'You seem to enjoy talking in riddles,' she snapped.

He made no answer but started forward on foot. The going grew difficult as the slope pitched steeply near the top, but finally he was able to belly down and wriggle forward to a point where he could see the dark dots of cabins against the white of the snow.

His glasses brought the camp into sharp focus. It took but a moment's looking for him to see that it was empty, that it had been empty for some time. No smoke came from any chimneys. There was no sign that the snow had been disturbed. They had moved out either before or during the early part of the storm. He could feel the dead, deserted air of the place like a blow.

Turning, he motioned to Lynn. He was mildly surprised when she came on, leading his two horses. When she reached him, he saw that his pack was still undisturbed. She said, 'I could have looked for my guns while you were gone.'

'And you would have if you'd thought you could find them before I came back and

127

caught you trying,' he jibed at her. He handed her the glasses.

She studied the emptiness below. 'Look at the snow,' she said. 'They must have gone last night or early this morning. But where? And why would they leave in a storm like this?'

Again Larabee was struck by her sincere bewilderment. But he continued to probe her. 'I thought you might be able to answer those questions.'

'They had to go west,' she said. 'If they'd followed the trail back toward Glory Hole, we'd have heard them. But how do they know this trail goes anywhere?'

'They know that,' Larabee assured her. 'They know that the trail will take them over into Idaho Territory—them and their string of mules loaded with boxes of Army ammunition.'

She started. 'Are you trying to tell me . . .? That's ridiculous! The Army had investigators all over this part of the country. They found nothing!' She swept out a hand. 'And what is your interest in those mules anyway, Mr. Larabee?'

'The Army found nothing because they didn't know what to look for,' Larabee said. 'I do now.' He started the chestnut forward. 'It's safe enough to go down.'

The trail widened as they went downslope and Lynn pulled alongside Larabee. Suddenly her sorrel seemed to lurch, so that it shouldered against the chestnut. She leaned out as if to grab Larabee. This time he was a second too late to catch the meaning of her movement.

When she straightened up, she held his .44 in her hand.

'Now, Mr. Larabee, maybe you'll stop being so secretive and answer my questions.'

Larabee grinned at her. 'They say a woman's curiosity is the strongest thing about her. Yours must be if you'd rather hear me talk than shoot me.'

'I can do that any time I choose,' she said evenly. 'Right now, I want to know who you are. And I want to know exactly what you're accusing me of. Because that's what you've been doing—accusing me.'

Larabee stared at the gun steady in her hand. 'The answers are right over that rise to the north,' he said. And swinging the chestnut, he started forward.

He was gambling, he knew. She could shoot him down instead of following him. But he counted on her curiosity and on whatever it was inside her that had held her back from killing him as soon as she'd taken the gun.

He could answer her questions, he thought. But by his thinking, that was a greater risk than riding on this way. Because if she heard his accusations before she saw the proof of what he had been claiming, then she just might flare up and pull that trigger.

She might anyway, he knew. If she was part of the gang as he'd once suspected her of being, if he was wrong about his change of mind these last hours, then she would shoot him.

One way or another, he judged that he had about one chance in five of staying alive for the next hour.

CHAPTER THIRTEEN

Lynn was not the kind who killed easily, Larabee thought as he put his back to her and rode off without looking around. And if he was right in thinking that, then the longer she held off using the gun, the better his chances of living were.

He led the way directly into the camp, dismounted, and walked into the largest cabin. Lynn stayed grimly, silently behind him. He put his hand on the cookstove. It was still faintly warm.

'They cooked a breakfast before they left,' he remarked. 'I'd guess the snow was already coming down when they started.'

'You're fishing for time, Mr. Larabee.'

'No,' he said, 'I'm building a case for my defense.' Returning to the chestnut, he mounted and rode to the far edge of the camp, where the snow-buried trail started up out of the hollow. Here he climbed down and brushed away a good four inches of snow. He nodded down at the clear sign of men and animals. Feet and hooves had packed and chewed those first inches of snow and then the later fall had come to hide them.

'If you can read sign,' Larabee said, 'you should be able to see that there's a lot of different kinds of hoofprints, more than saddle and pack horses can account for.'

'If you mean some of those are mule prints, I can't tell any difference.'

Larabee shrugged and turned, studying the way the land lay between the camp and the ridge behind which Barling said was the opening to the tunnel. He said, 'They'll have brought the mules down that pitch about this angle.' He began walking, leading the chestnut and the bay, letting her follow on the sorrel. Now and then he stopped to brush away snow, revealing the sign beneath the heavy, wet upper layer. At the top of the ridge, he stopped and waited for her. There was no need to continue tracing the mules' line of march. Straight across the ridge loomed a high wall of rock, and cut into its face was the wide opening of the tunnel mouth. And even from here, the pungent smell of recently used blasting powder and the sharp tang of a closed-in barn came strongly to their nostrils.

Wordlessly, Lynn untied her pack animal and tossed the reins to Larabee. Then she spurred the sorrel down the slope and across to the tunnel mouth. He watched her disappear inside. A few moments later she came out again and spurred her horse alongside him.

'Where does it go?'

Larabee climbed onto the chestnut. 'According to Barling, it cuts all the way through that rock mountain and comes out in the canyon Dan Peters was exploring the day he was shot. I suspect it's either an ancient geological fault or an old watercourse that found softer rock to burrow through.'

She hardly seemed to hear his last words. She said, 'And you claim that Dan came into the tunnel, found the mules, and was shot by the raiders?' She paused and added, 'Kessler's miners?'

'I don't know who shot Dan,' Larabee confessed. 'But I doubt if he walked through the tunnel. Barling told me that the last time he saw the other side, a spring flood had covered the opening with washed down rubble. My guess is that the raiders opened it up just enough to run the mules through from that end, blocked it off again, and then blocked this end off as well, leaving themselves only enough opening to get feed and water in to the stock. Today, they blasted all the rock out of this end, packed the mule train, and started it west.'

She remained out of arm's reach of him, the gun still steady in her hand. Larabee said dryly, 'Aren't you being a little foolish? When you rode off to look over the tunnel, you left me with my carbine in its saddle boot. I could have used it on you easily enough when you came out of the dark into the daylight.'

She flushed. 'It seems that I'm not very used to this kind of work, doesn't it?' He saw her mouth tremble, and for the first time since he had caught her at her camp, it struck him that she had been suppressing her emotions with what must have been a tremendous effort.

He said gently, 'If you were still as convinced that I'd killed Dan, you wouldn't have made that mistake. All right, then you have some doubts about my being a killer. I'll match you, and have doubts about your being in with the raiders.'

She gasped. 'I? What reason could you have—could anyone have—for thinking that I would involve myself in something like that!'

Now he could see the anger working up in her again. He said quickly, 'A number of reasons. I suggested them to Dan. That's why he got mad at me. But you can believe me when I tell you that he calmed down the same night. And later he did a little thinking about you, and a little asking too.'

She let the gun drop into her lap and squeezed her hands tightly over the saddlehorn. 'So that's why he was asking me all those questions about my financial state and about where I'd been before I came to Glory Hole.'

'Don't blame him,' Larabee said. 'He was doing a job. He'd been shirking it because he loved you. After I came, he had to face up to it.'

'Why?' she cried. 'What kind of job was he doing that would make him think that I—'

Larabee interrupted her sharply. 'He was a

Pinkerton man, hired by the government to help get at the bottom of the raids.' Quickly now, he sketched out for her the relationship of the raids and their meaning to the potential peace of this part of the West.

'And you?' she demanded. 'Who are you that Dan would—would stop shirking his job, as you put it, when you came?'

'I'm a Cavalry officer,' Larabee said. He explained his job to her. 'That's why Barling was willing to help me, after I proved myself to him.' He added lightly, 'I can do the same with you when we make camp, if you still don't believe me.'

She was slumped in the saddle now, her thoughts obviously not on his words. She whispered, 'Dan must have died thinking that I—I was one of them!'

'No,' Larabee lied. 'Before we parted that last morning, he made it clear he was convinced that you weren't. He had me over half convinced too.'

He saw a relaxing of her body, an easing of the stricken expression on her features. She was silent a moment, pulling together her strength. Finally she said, 'If you didn't kill Dan and if the raiders didn't—who could have?'

'Someone he didn't expect to,' Larabee said. 'I've given it a lot of thought. Dan was a trained man. If he'd seen anyone he suspected at all, he wouldn't have let them get the drop on him. So it must have been someone he didn't even think to protect himself from. Someone he trusted.'

She touched her tongue to her lips. 'Someone like me or Brooks or you?'

'Or Barling or his law partner,' Larabee said. 'Not men like Kessler and Briggs. Kessler was in the hospital. I put him there so he couldn't bother us. And Dan wouldn't have let Briggs get within shooting range of him.' He looked up at the sky, noting that the snow had stopped for the time being.

'I can't imagine old Elston or Barling being involved,' Larabee said. 'I know it wasn't myself, and I'm growing more sure of you all the time.'

'That leaves Brooks,' she said. 'I can't believe that. Why would he? He has money, reputation, a fine future in politics and business . . .'

Larabee told her what Peters had reported about Reardon's financial problems. 'My guess is that he tapped his bank—and every other source he could—to speculate on that railroad land. When the company delayed building until the Indian troubles were settled, Reardon was caught in a trap.' He paused, adding, 'Remember, he followed you last night and then came on here. He either put wings on his horse and flew back to Glory Hole or he's still with the raiders. And if he's with them, it's because he's making sure that the ammunition gets to the main cache, to join the guns he has there.'

She drew a deep breath. 'If this is true, what are you going to do?'

'Follow them,' Larabee said. 'Follow and find out where they're taking the ammunition. Once I do, then I'll go to the nearest Army post and have the troops move in.'

'And you don't think they'll find out you're following?' She was almost sarcastic now. 'You don't think they'll try to stop you?'

'I'm sure they will,' Larabee said blandly. 'And I can't think of a better reason for you to give me back my gun.'

She stared at him. 'And then what do I do?'

'Stay here and wait for a chinook. When it comes, you can go back through the tunnel to the canyon country. It'll be muddy but passable.'

'No,' she said flatly. 'If you're right, Brooks killed Dan. Or one of the raiders killed him. Either way, I came here to find the man who murdered my—my future husband. I told you before that I don't give up easily.'

She had picked up the gun again, and Larabee said dryly, 'I don't seem to be in a position to argue. But you pointed out yourself that they'll try to stop me. Do you think they'd hesitate in stopping you because you're a woman?'

'No,' she admitted. She looked down at the gun. 'I think I believe you, Mr. Larabee, enough anyway to make a truce with you. I'll trade your gun for my two. We'll trust each other for our mutual protection. And because we both have reason to follow the mule train. But I'm reserving my full belief until you've either proved what you claim or until I've learned you're lying to me.'

'A fair enough deal, if your word is better than it was last night.'

She flushed again. 'Last night I was—as you pointed out—using a woman's weapons. And last night I wasn't faced with knowing that the raiders have been here, that they are probably ahead of us, and that they might try to kill me as well as you.'

She took a deep breath. 'I'm a businesswoman, not a gambler. Two of us have more chance of survival than one. I don't intend to try to trick you again.'

She handed him his gun, butt first. Holstering it, Larabee undid one rope on his pack, lifted a flap, and brought out her carbine and thirty-eight. He handed them to her.

'They were within my reach all of the time!' She laughed suddenly. 'You're very clever, Mr. Larabee—or is it Captain or . . .'

'Major,' he said. 'But since my work requires me to keep my Cavalry connections a secret, I'd prefer for you to forget it. And we haven't time for formalities. My first name is Clint.'

'As you wish,' she said stiffly. The laughter

was gone. It was obvious to Larabee that she had put her mind back on the problem ahead of them. 'How far ahead will they be?'

He said, 'Eight or nine men, one of them still badly bruised, pack horses and a string of loaded mules: they won't make much time even on a clear trail.' He glanced at the sky. It was a dull, lowering gray, but still holding its snow.

'I'd guess that we'll find they've broken trail for us within a mile or so. We'll have that advantage until it snows again.'

'In other words, you aren't in any hurry to start after them right away.'

'No,' he agreed. 'Let them get enough of a start so we won't trample on their heels. We can use the time to rest the horses and have a hot meal. Even at that, we should catch up with them by the time they make camp tonight.'

'As you wish, Major.' Reining her sorrel around, she rode for the deserted cabins.

CHAPTER FOURTEEN

Larabee stopped on a low rise and studied the landscape ahead. Old Sawtooth was at their backs now, the trail having led them around from its north to its west face. From his vantage point, Larabee could see the dark, thin line of the mule train against the white of the snow. Well beyond where the front of the dark line disappeared into a mass of timber, the mountains squeezed together to form a narrow notch.

Larabee pointed out the notch to Lynn. 'My guess is that they'll work as close as they can to the foot of the pass by tomorrow evening. Then the next morning, they'll try to fight their way across before dark.'

'How long do you think it will take them to reach the foot of the pass?' she asked.

Larabee tried to measure the distance by eye. The going was achingly slow for the mule train and its handlers. In the past two days, another eight inches of snow had fallen, and every foot of trail had to be broken by a horse and rider. Even following along on the already broken trail, Larabee could tell how much had been taken out of the chestnut and the sorrel and the pack animals. He suspected that, take turns as they might, Kessler's crew's horses must be near exhaustion.

'I'd give them until tomorrow night,' Larabee said. 'If another big storm doesn't hit, they should be on the other side of the pass two nights from now.'

'And then?'

'I've been through the country on the other side,' he answered. 'An old gold prospectors' trail angles south along the western slope of the mountains. About a day's ride the other side of the notch, there's an abandoned gold camp. Beyond that, there are two trails. The one that looks good is impassable because the bridges over deep canyons fell in a few years back. The other one is fair enough for men on horseback or pack animals, but it takes some finding.'

Lynn said impatiently, 'Just how far ahead are you going to let them get, Major?'

'Near enough to be caught but not so close they can catch us,' he answered. 'And forget the Major.'

'I might, if I ever find out you've told me the truth,' she replied. 'But for two days we've got no closer than this. How do I know that Brooks is with them? And if he is, how do I know he isn't Kessler's prisoner? You could be in with Kessler, and doing this to make sure I don't get away and warn the Army about the mule train.'

'What do you want—to ride up and talk to Reardon and Kessler?' Larabee demanded.

'I want to get close enough to have a chance

141

to see and hear them,' she snapped.

Larabee stifled a desire to comment on stubborn females. But he had to admit she hadn't been any great hindrance to him since they'd left the miners' camp. She hadn't been comfortable company either, he thought. She made it plain enough that for all the proof he had shown her, she wasn't yet willing to be convinced that he was what he claimed to be. At the same time, the more he saw and heard her, the more certain he became that she was innocent. He tried to make their relationship a more pleasant one, free of tension, but she refused to accept any friendly overtures on his part. She had used the right word back there at the camp when she'd said she would make a truce with him. And that was all it was; she gave of herself no more than that.

'All right,' Larabee said. 'They'll be over a rise before long. Then we can come out of this timber and move on.' He looked up at the sky, which still remained a dirty, oppressive gray squashing down on them. 'If it doesn't start snowing hard, we can be on their heels by dark. Then it will depend on where they make camp as to how close we can get to them.'

She nodded but said nothing. Finally the last of the long, dark string disappeared and Larabee sent the chestnut out into the open and down the slope ahead. They were able to make fair time with all but the most recent inch of snow packed down by the horses and mules ahead of them. Even so, the terrain almost defeated them. In many places it was flat and open so that they had to stop and wait at the edge of a patch of timber until the mule train went out of sight around a turn or over a ridge.

Larabee realized Lynn's growing impatience, but he also knew that he wasn't dealing with fools. He was dealing with men who had made four successful raids against trained Cavalrymen. And they hadn't got away with all those guns and ammunition and supplies by making foolish mistakes. As he said finally to her, 'Kessler won't overlook dropping a man back as a watchdog. Right now, I'm pretty sure they can't guess how close we are. But I am sure they know we're on their trail. So don't misjudge him—or we could ride into an ambush and end up dead in this snow.'

'Are you trying to frighten me, Major?'

'No, just trying to take that sour expression from your face.'

She stared at him as if she wanted to answer, but then she turned silently away. They rode without speaking, the tension building between them until it became a tangible thing to Larabee. Finally the country broke up, the trail rising and falling and twisting abruptly. Now they could make faster time, not having to worry too much about being seen from any great distance ahead.

The early, cloudy dark came down swiftly,

and with it the snow began to fall again—a thick, blinding blanket. Larabee swore to himself as he ducked his head against the cold slap of the wet flakes.

'Do you think they'll have gone much farther?' Lynn asked.

He squinted ahead. The mule train had disappeared beyond a sharp, steep rise not too far beyond them. To the left the slope of the mountains squeezed down and sent out a spur that ran into the rise.

'They'll be camping now if there's any likely place,' he decided. 'The country's getting too rugged to risk pushing tired animals in the dark and the snow.'

A short distance on, Larabee reined in and squinted again, but this time toward the mountain face looming on the left. 'There's a lot of rock over there,' he said. 'I'm going to see if there aren't some sheltered places where we can hole up.' He pointed to the side. 'Pull the horses into that timber while I ride over and see what I can find.'

Leaving her, he angled the chestnut along the slope of the rise. Now, with no broken trail underfoot, it tired quickly. Finally Larabee left it to rest and pushed his way forward on foot. He caught the sound of water falling and came to a creek invisible but busy under the snow. He followed along it until he reached a waterfall dropping down through the white curtain from some unknown distance above.

To the south of the waterfall, at the base of the spur running out from the rock face of the mountain, he found what he sought: an overhang where they could build a fire and stay dry as long as no wind came up to blow the snow at them. A short way farther along, he located a deeper recess with a spring oozing through the snow at one side of the opening.

Wearily, he slogged back to the chestnut and returned to where he had left Lynn. The pack animals were standing under the shelter of a bristly spruce but she and her sorrel were gone. Crawling down from the saddle, Larabee went onto the trail and studied what sign was still visible under the rapidly falling snow.

Straightening up, he swore angrily. The fool! She had ridden after the mule train. Going, he guessed, to the top of the ridge in the hope of seeing where Kessler and his men were camped. He turned to go back to the horses and saw her coming, a suddenly looming shape in the darkness and snow.

'That was a crazy thing to do,' he snapped. 'They could have a guard posted just to watch for someone coming up behind them!'

'They did,' she answered him. Her voice held a thread of self-satisfaction. 'You do your part, Major, and I'll do mine. And I'm not a complete idiot. I didn't ride in the middle of the trail all the way, you know. I went through the timber on foot the last hundred yards or so. There's a lone guard under some rocks at the top of the ridge. Their camp is just down the other side. I could see the fires.'

'Right now,' Larabee answered, 'I'm only interested in our own fire.' He started the chestnut back along the path he had made earlier, leaving her to bring the pack animals.

It wasn't until they had the gear unloaded and the horses in the recess by the small spring and their own camp set up that Larabee paused long enough to look at Lynn. For the first time he was struck by how keyed up she must be. Weariness cut deeply into her handsome features. Yet she worked with a kind of determined frenzy, as if every moment now was precious.

While he took care of their gear and the animals, she had gathered wood and started a small fire, placing it so that the heat bounced off the rear of the overhang and from the side walls to encase them in warmth on three sides. Now she was swiftly getting their meal ready.

He said gently, 'We have all night. You'll collapse if you don't slow down.'

She stopped abruptly and slumped to a small rock. She began to cry soundlessly, her face buried in her hands, her body humped over. Larabee started toward her and then discreetly let her have her privacy. He finished setting up their camp and then took over the chore of the cooking.

She rose suddenly and walked away into the night. She came back, brushing snow from her hair, her face rosy from being washed in icy water.

'I'm sorry,' she said simply. 'But I kept thinking that if you're right, Dan's murderer must be just over the ridge from me.'

'Riding this kind of trail isn't easy for anyone,' Larabee said. 'But thinking that way won't make it any easier for you. Put your mind on something else.'

'Yes, doctor,' she mocked softly. Then she was silent again.

Larabee had set her tent up at the far side of the overhang. As soon as she'd eaten and cleaned up her plate and utensils, she disappeared inside the tent. It was too small to contain all of her bedroll, and soon Larabee could see the end of it bulge out as she slid her feet down to the end. A little later he went near the tent and listened to her steady, tired breathing. She was already asleep.

Quietly, he cleaned up the cooking pans, had a pipe with the last of the coffee, and then went out to make a final check of the horses. The snow was coming down violently now, wiping out his tracks almost as fast as he made them. At least, he thought, Kessler wouldn't learn anything by sending a man back to hunt for their sign—not in a storm like this.

Rolling into his blankets, he fell asleep quickly. The first hint of daylight brought him awake and stiffly to his feet. The fire was higher than he expected it to be and for a moment he thought Lynn must already be up. But a glance at the tent showed him the bulge of her feet in the bedroll. *Let her sleep,* he thought. Pulling on his boots, he set water on to boil and left the overhang to tend the horses.

He stopped abruptly. The snow had thinned to an occasional flake drifting from the lightening sky. And without any wind, there was nothing to cover the fresh tracks of Lynn's boots. He hurried back to the tent and bent, squeezing the lump he had taken for her feet. It was soft, no more than a mound of clothing stuffed down there. Swearing now, he hurried to the recess and the horses.

The sorrel was gone. Larabee went outside and let his eyes follow the line of tracks marking its path. There was no doubt about it. Lynn was heading straight for the raiders' camp.

CHAPTER FIFTEEN

Swearing softly, Larabee started to feed and water the horses. He grunted as he realized the chore had already been done. His first thought had been that she had ridden to join the raiders, and to warn them of his being so close. Now he wondered just what she was up to.

The answer came quickly, frighteningly: the stubborn idiot was carrying out her threat of trying to sneak up on their camp to see if she couldn't overhear something. Which meant, he thought sourly, that she still refused to believe him. She wouldn't accept his story until she heard with her own ears—and she would have to hear the truth from Brooks Reardon, Larabee suspected.

He lifted his saddle, ready to put it on the chestnut and go after her, when the sound of hooves crunching snow took him to the front of the recess. She came riding to him, her cheeks bright with color from the frosty air, her eyes sparkling. She was a changeable creature, he thought. She wasn't just smiling a good morning at him—she was laughing!

'And here I thought my breakfast would be all ready for me.'

'How close did you get?' he demanded.

'Close enough to hear them but not close

enough to be seen by their guard,' she answered. She continued to laugh. 'Don't worry, Major—Clint, I mean. They don't have any idea how close we are. The snow has been good to us that way, covering our tracks better than it has theirs.'

'Except the ones you made this morning,' Larabee said bluntly.

'I'm sorry to disappoint you, but I didn't take the sorrel anywhere near the trail. I found a nice protected stretch of timber that left no sign at all.'

Still angry, Larabee took the reins of her horse while she dismounted. Then he unsaddled the sorrel and returned to their camp. She had gone ahead and was cooking breakfast when he arrived. In his few moments alone he had found time to realize the implication in her calling him something other than Major.

He said as she dished up the food, 'So you heard the truth.'

'Yes,' she said. The laughter left her momentarily. 'Maybe I'm strange, or crazy. But when I heard enough to know that you had told me the truth, I felt—well, free. Even seeing Brooks there and knowing now that he was the one who shot Dan hasn't taken that feeling away.'

Larabee said gently, 'When you're in a spot like this, you have to live for the present. You can't live in the past. And right now, being able to trust me is more important to you than revenge.'

She poured the coffee. 'I'm glad you understand,' she said. 'Maybe the feeling won't last. I don't know. I didn't have my carbine with me—I left it on the sorrel—or I might have shot at Brooks.' She paused and added, 'I may yet.'

'If we win, you can be sure he'll hang,' Larabee said. 'That should be enough for you.'

She shook her head. 'I wish I knew. I won't let myself think about it. Not now.'

Sensing that she was losing her mood of pleasure, Larabee said, 'What did you hear? Have they gone?'

'They will be by the time we're through eating.' She nodded in the direction of the trail. 'I didn't get too close, but the wind was blowing just right to bring the talk to me. Brooks and Kessler were arguing. Kessler wanted to stay here until the sky cleared. But Brooks insisted they go on. He's worried about your being close and he's anxious to get the ammunition to the main cache. He wants to make a deal before winter sets in and he might be forced to wait until spring to get his money.'

'That means the Indians will be ready for war when spring does come,' Larabee said tiredly.

'He sounded very sure of that,' she admitted. She sipped her coffee. 'Anyway, Brooks won the argument. He's obviously the leader.'

'Did you actually hear him say that he killed Dan Peters?'

Her expression clouded. 'No, but Kessler made a remark about it and Brooks didn't make any denial.'

Again Larabee hurriedly shifted the subject. He said, 'Reardon is right, of course. With the pass just ahead, they'd be foolish to stay here any longer than necessary, even if we weren't behind them.'

'They don't seem to know that I'm with you,' she said. 'I got the feeling that Brooks thinks you might have talked your way out of being suspected for Dan's murder and sent me back to Barling to get a posse or go warn the Army—if I found you at all. That's why he's in such a terrible hurry: he isn't sure how many are behind them or if there'll be troops waiting on the other side of the mountains.'

Larabee grinned. 'Let him wriggle,' he said. He added, 'When this is over, I think I'll recommend you for a Cavalry commission. You'd make a good agent.'

She laughed. 'My thoughts were running in a different direction. I was thinking what a fine little hotel I could build here. I might even have a whole string of overnight stops just waiting for people like you to come along.'

'So you could charge room rent?'

'Of course. I'm a businesswoman, remember.'

152

He made himself keep up the light tone with her, even though his mind wanted to work on the problem of what lay ahead. Finally, when they were ready for the trail, she dropped into a more serious mood.

'I took a look at the country from the ridge to the pass,' she said. 'There are some places where we might be able to ride around and get ahead of them.'

'I can't risk going in front,' he said. 'They just might know of a short-cut route once they're over the pass. If I lose them, I'll lose my chance of locating the main cache.'

She nodded, understanding. Mounting her sorrel, she tied her pack horse on behind and started along the trail she had broken earlier. Larabee, on the chestnut, followed, his mind still working on the problem that lay ahead of them. When they neared the trail, he stopped her and had her hold the horses while he climbed the ridge on foot and surveyed the spread of land ahead. As he had hoped, the raiders were well along toward the pass. The long train of mules and horses made a thin, dark line against the snow. Even as he watched, they disappeared into a thick stand of timber. Larabee waited, looking for a drag rider who might be looking for him. But he saw no one and so he returned to Lynn.

'We can risk the trail now.'

It was slow going, with Larabee and the chestnut having to break through the snow

153

that had fallen during the night. But once they reached the point where the raiders had made camp, the snow was well packed, making travel easier. Larabee had to slow their pace, not wanting to get too close to the rear of the train.

At one point, they topped a rise just as the sun broke through the cloud layer. A chill north wind stirred the air, making Lynn pull her shoulders together. Larabee pointed toward the pass, close enough now for them to see clearly the trail as it left the timber and climbed through barren country. The pass itself was marked by a wide notch set between towering peaks.

'Once we get above timberline, the real risk begins,' Larabee said flatly. 'All they need to do is post a lookout at the top of the pass, and they most likely will if they figure I'm behind them. We don't even dare to go much farther today. They'll be over the top before dark, and a man looking back in this clearing air can see anything that moves.'

'But can we risk waiting until they get on the other side?' she wondered.

'We have to,' he said. 'And that's another problem. We don't know what kind of weather there's been over there. The snow could be thinner, or there might be none at all. If the going is easy for them—or if they know a special trail—they have a good chance of losing us.'

'No,' she said with sudden savagery. 'I told you that I'm not a gambler. And that's true. But I won't take a chance on letting Dan's killer get away free!'

'You don't want him caught any more than I do,' Larabee answered. He paused and studied the stretch of timber, the rising mountains, capped by the barren country and then the notch set against the now solid blue of the sky. 'We've got one chance to make sure they don't get away from us.'

She waited, and he said, 'We'll go down into that next patch of timber and make camp. We'll get as much rest as we can and then make our run in the dark.'

She looked up at the blue sky. 'There'll be a piece of moon tonight.'

'By the time it rises, let's hope we're over the top and down into the timber.'

Pulling well off the trail and behind a rise, Larabee built a small fire. After a quick meal, they slept. Larabee awoke to find dusk settling. Overhead, the first stars were beginning to show in the deep purple of the sky. A cold wind ruffled the trees around them, making him think just how icy this night's ride would be.

He wakened Lynn and let her prepare a small meal while he readied the horses. They gulped down coffee and stick bread, mounted their horses and started for the notch.

The trail was well packed here and they moved at an even, steady pace through the deepening darkness. As the pitch steepened, the horses slowed, but Larabee felt no sign of the chestnut tiring and so he kept it moving. He hesitated as they reached the end of the timber.

'Keep one hand close to your carbine,' he said quietly, and rode into the open.

The trail was crisp and clear—a dark line showing against the white of the snow. Here the wind was sharp, cutting against their right sides. Larabee fought down a temptation to push the horses, to reach the notch as fast as possible.

The trail seemed to kink back and forth endlessly, but they finally came to the flat stretch that led through the notch. Once into it, the bite of the wind lessened. The chestnut seemed to relax, and Larabee slapped it on the neck. 'Not yet, boy,' he said softly. 'Don't ease up quite yet.'

To Lynn, he said, 'There's no place to hide. We'll just have to chance their having left a man up here.'

She nodded silently and reached out, putting a hand on the butt of her carbine. They moved on at the same pace. Suddenly the rock walls of the notch ended. The wind came from a different quarter here and there was the feeling of wetness in it again. But overhead the stars still showed brightly, and to the east they could see the first hint of the rising moon.

Larabee paused now and pointed downslope. 'There's more snow here than we had,' he said. 'That can help us as long as we stay on the trail they've broken for us. But if we're seen and have to break for it, we could get in trouble.'

'You worry too much,' she said.

'No,' Larabee corrected her, 'I just try to plan for anything that might happen.' He moved his frozen face muscles in a travesty of a smile. 'Right now, I'm planning to reach that timber downslope and get in front of a fire.'

'Doesn't that depend on how far they got before they made camp?'

He pointed again. 'If you look closely, you can see a flicker every now and then—about a mile down. That'll be from their fire. We can camp at this end of the timber and be almost half a mile away.'

He started the chestnut down the slope. The trail curved, making a switch toward the timber. It kinked back the other way and then toward the timber once more. Then it broke onto the level of a long flat so that they were no longer riding downslope. The moon came up, behind their left shoulders now. The timber still seemed an endless distance away and the moonlight was growing brighter, outlining them in this open landscape.

Around them was a jumble of rocks and the first scrubby trees. On the right it seemed to end abruptly, at the lip of a canyon, Larabee guessed. On the left the rocks tumbled to the base of the mountains rising starkly against the sky.

The first shot was a shock. It cracked on the icy night and against Larabee's ears just as the sound of lead slapping into the bay's pack came. Larabee swore and jerked the chestnut at the same time as he reached for his carbine.

'Into the rocks!' he ordered.

A second shot came, and then a third on its heels, both kicking snow by the feet of their horses. But now they were in the jumble of rock on the right side of the trail and after two more futile shots, the raiders were suddenly quiet.

Larabee pulled up behind a massive boulder. 'They're right where the timber thickens,' he said bitterly. 'And I judge two at the very least.'

'And no way around from here,' Lynn added quietly.

'No way at all this far up,' he said. 'A ways down, I know how to bypass them. I spent some time in that country. But up here, we're trapped. We can't go forward and we can't go back without exposing ourselves. We can't do anything but sit and wait.'

'And freeze to death,' Lynn added in the same quiet voice.

CHAPTER SIXTEEN

Larabee studied the bleak landscape around them. The drop-off on their right was marked by an uneven line of moonlit snow contrasting with deep blackness. He glanced to the left, debating their chances of crossing the trail and finding safety closer to the mountains.

There might be a chance, he thought, if— Lynn's calm voice interrupted his thoughts. 'Three or four men just crossed to the other side of the trail. I'm sure that one of them was Brooks.'

Larabee stopped considering crossing the trail. He moved closer to where she stood and peered around the big rock at the terrain below. For a moment he could hear only the heavy breathing of their horses, and then he caught the crackle of a foot pressing down on a thin crust of ice, the clatter of a horseshoe against cold rock and, closer than he liked, the snort of a horse.

'They're working up through the rocks on both sides of the trail,' he said. 'They'll try to pin us here from both sides and then work someone behind us.'

Lynn hefted her rifle. 'Can't we do something? Do we have to wait here to be slaughtered like cattle? Like Dan was?'

'No,' Larabee said. He framed his thoughts slowly into words, planning this as he talked. 'There's one possible chance. But it could mean a big risk for you.'

'Bigger than staying here and waiting?' she demanded tartly. 'Oh, I know. You want me to try to ride back while you cover me, and end up sacrificing yourself.'

'I had more in mind your giving yourself up,' Larabee said. He spoke with quick urgency now as the ideas came almost faster than he could get them out. When he finished, he added, 'It's the only chance I can see. If it doesn't work, we're no worse off. If it does, I just might be able to do something.'

She wasted little time considering his plan. She said, 'If I can act well enough, Brooks just might believe me.' She smiled wryly. 'And you have a point: he is convinced that my first interest is business.'

'Kessler might not be so easy to fool,' Larabee said.

She shrugged. 'If Brooks accepts me, I'll risk Kessler.' She paused as rock rattled almost directly across the trail from them. 'We'll have to hurry.'

Nodding, Larabee climbed down from the chestnut and led it, with the bay trailing along, in a twisting path through the rocks until he could see the ragged rim of the drop-off. He paused and waited for Lynn to catch up. Now he left the horses with her and started hunting.

He was seeking three things: a deep recess created by some of the huge boulders meeting at their tops, a smaller rock balanced on top of a larger one with both close to the drop-off, and finally a small tree he could break a branch from to use to brush out his tracks.

He found the recess and quickly put his two horses inside. While he was hunting for one rock balanced on another, he found the tree he sought. Breaking off a branch, he carefully smoothed away the sign of his having led the horses into the recess. Then he returned to his searching. He could hear them maneuvering close below and not too far to the left and urgency drove him to digging up a small boulder and somehow finding the strength to maneuver it to the top of a flat-surfaced rock at the very edge of the drop-off. He clambered after it and lay, catching his breath. He looked down at Lynn, wondering what would happen if he'd been wrong about her all along, if she was really clever enough to have fooled him as he now planned for her to fool Reardon.

There was only one way to find out. 'Get set,' he panted.

She nodded and raised her carbine. Her lips framed the words, 'Good luck, Clint.' She raised her voice so that it carried on the clear, cold night. 'And now what are you going to do, Major?' Her voice mocked him. 'Didn't you think I'd be clever enough to find a way to get my guns back?'

Larabee answered, 'Don't be a fool, Miss Graham. So far there are no charges against you. Don't do something you can't buy your way out of. Now put that carbine down!'

'Get back!' she cried, filling her voice with shrill fear. She lifted her gun.

Larabee stared at the barrel aimed almost directly at him. Then it swung slightly to one side. She fired, and the sound was a sharp hammer blow on the night air.

Larabee let the echo of the shot begin to fade and then he cried out as a man in fear and pain would. Bending, he lifted the small boulder. Lynn fired again. Larabee gave a grunt and heaved the rock out toward the drop-off. It struck the edge and bounced off into space. The sound of its crashing was louder than the shot had been. Larabee screamed, letting the sound tail off to grow fainter and fainter.

Lynn cried, 'No! Oh, no!' She ran to the edge of the drop-off. 'Major? Major . . .' Her voice burbled away to silence.

Larabee quickly slid down from the rock and walked heavily to the drop-off. Stepping carefully to one side, he worked his way to the recess, brushing out his tracks as he went. He huddled inside, drawing warmth from the horses, a hand over each of their muzzles, and listened as well as he could to what went on outside.

Lynn was riding back toward the trail now,

he thought, hearing the crackle of hooves on frozen snow. Soon she would have to face Reardon. He only hoped that the cold air would carry the sound of their voices this far.

A rifle shot cracked on the air. Lynn cried, 'Brooks, stop shooting! It's me, Lynn!' Larabee could have sworn that she was sobbing as she talked.

And then Reardon's voice: 'What is this, Lynn? What the devil are you doing here?'

'Larabee brought me,' she answered. Her sobbing had stopped and there was savagery in her voice now. 'I went after him, to kill him for shooting Dan. He trapped me and made me come with him.' She gave a bitter laugh. 'This morning I learned why he made me come along.'

'Ah?' Reardon's voice was thick with skepticism.

'This morning he took me where I could see your camp, and you. And he told me that I was his insurance against your attacking us.'

'Larabee doesn't know me very well, does he?' Reardon said dryly.

'He didn't believe you'd shoot at a woman,' Lynn said.

'My dear, how was I to know you were with him? I assumed that when the snow came, you'd give up your chase and turn back.' Now his voice was smooth, almost soothing. He added in a different tone, 'And even after you learned what I'm up to, you wanted to get away from Larabee and join me? Why, Lynn?'

'You have a good deal more to offer, Brooks. To be blunt, I want a share in your profits.'

Kessler's deep voice rumbled out, 'Watch her, Reardon!'

'I'm no fool,' Reardon snapped. He laughed suddenly. 'But then Lynn always was a little greedy . . .' He broke off and started again. 'I'm sorry, my dear. There isn't profit enough for us all.'

Larabee held his breath. This was the test. If Reardon accepted what Lynn was supposed to say next, then this plan had a chance of working.

She said, 'There'd be more than enough for us all, if you got nearly double what you could normally expect to get.'

'I told you I was no fool,' Reardon snapped at her.

'Nor am I,' she answered levelly. 'I learned a lot from Larabee these last few days, Brooks— about Indians and which ones are the most restless, the most badly armed, the richest.'

There was a long silence. Then Reardon said so softly Larabee barely heard the words, 'Ride this way with your hands high, Lynn. Kessler, take a couple of men and go have a look around where she was when she did that shooting. Let's make sure Larabee went to join Dan Peters.'

'Get some lanterns,' Kessler shouted. To

Reardon, he said, 'I still say this could be a trap.'

'Of course,' Lynn said, 'one powerful woman against nine weak, armed men!'

Reardon said, 'If you see anything suspicious start shooting. I'll take Lynn back to camp and see if I can't thaw a little more interesting information from her.'

Larabee clamped his hands tightly over the horses' muzzles as he heard riders coming toward him. He could feel the chill creeping through his body as he held himself and the horses motionless. The search party passed within yards of him and went on.

He heard Kessler say, 'By God, something went over the edge right enough.' He laughed. 'And from the way Reardon says that woman took out after Larabee when she thought he'd killed Peters, maybe she did shoot him. She's long enough on nerve.'

'I don't like it,' Briggs said. 'That Larabee ain't nobody's fool neither.'

'Just in case he ain't dead, we'll keep some men hanging back,' Kessler said. 'All right, let's go get warm. Those ribs of mine are aching again.' He added savagely, 'I just hope Larabee is still alive. I'd like one more good chance at him!'

Larabee listened to them riding away. The night grew still. Even the wind had dropped. Finally he risked freeing the horses and leading them into the open. Cautiously, he worked his way to the edge of the trail and looked around, his head cocked for strange sounds. But there were none and so he crossed to the left side and began a slow, twisting journey to the beginning of the bluffs that marked the mountains.

Finding a deep recess, he risked a small fire to thaw himself and the horses out. He cooked and ate as much food as his stomach could hold and then rolled into his blankets for a short sleep.

The moon was still high in the sky when he came awake, ate the remains of his last meal, and readied the horses for the trail. He padded their harness and readied some wrappers for their hooves. Then he set off to work his way through the rocks and the timber below them until he was well beyond the raiders' camp. When he judged he was nearly opposite it, he took the time to wrap the hooves of both horses. Now he was in the forest and he had to work back and forth, keeping under those trees that had let the least snow through onto the ground. Elsewhere, the drifts were too deep for him to buck easily.

The going was slow, but by daylight he was able to pause at the top of a ridge and look back down the trail. He nodded in satisfaction at the sight of the mule train. He had put a good two miles between it and himself. Turning again into the woods, he resumed his slow back and forth trekking.

By evening, he judged he had a half day's march on the raiders. He made camp again in a recess in the rocky cliffs, and by daybreak was in the saddle and moving forward. Finally he crossed a low divide and saw country that he knew fairly well.

Ahead he could see the rolling sagelands of the high plains of this part of Idaho Territory. To his right, the mountains folded in layers with long valleys slashing in a generally northerly direction. To his left lay the still formidable upthrust of this end of the Bitterroots. And behind was the bitterly cold, snow-filled country he had slogged his way through.

There was snow ahead too, but it lay in great drifts against anything that had been in the path of what must have been scouring winds. And where there were no obstacles, barren rock could be seen. The sun, warmer at this lower latitude, had even made the snow sag in places, so that where it crested on the tops of protected ridges, it seemed ready to tumble down.

He rode openly on the trail now, wanting them to know that he was ahead—or that someone was. At the foot of the long grade that dropped from the divide, the trail branched. The wider one went temptingly southwest, down toward the open country hazy in the distance, and down toward the lava rock lands that shot long fingers into the southerly running bottoms of the mountains. Larabee knew that if the cache was in those lava lands, then Reardon would most likely turn down that wider trail.

Unless, Larabee thought, he knew that it was impassable some distance beyond. Impassable except to those who knew the secret of the five canyons. The smaller trail was the one Larabee wanted to keep the raiders from taking. It looked uninviting at first, starting off as it did in a north-westerly direction. But not too far along it made a sharp westerly and then southerly pair of bends. It too came out in the lava rock country and it did so by avoiding the collapsed bridges, the rock slides, and the five canyons that made the wider trail useless to the uninitiated.

His job then, he knew, was to get them onto the wider trail. And from there into his trap. He rode down the wide trail until he reached a level bench thick with timber. Here he laboriously chopped a half dozen trees, felling them so that they made an effective—and obviously recent—blockade. That done, he took to the timber and made a wide swing that carried him to the narrower trail. Whenever he could, he rode through snow, leaving as clear a set of tracks as he could manage. Reaching the trail, he rode down it to a place he recalled. He sighed with relief when he saw that his memory hadn't tricked him. Here the narrow trail went through high bluffs topped with trees. It was in his mind to work free the snow-soaked ground around the base of some of those trees, sending them down to fill the cut and effectively block the trail.

He backtracked and made camp long enough to eat and feed the horses. Then he tackled the job of trying to bring down the trees with nothing more than his folding Cavalry shovel. He dared not use his ax: the trees must look as if a storm had sent them crashing into the cut.

Twice he stopped to return to his camp, thaw out, and warm his insides with coffee. The moon was far up in the sky when the first tree crashed into the cut. Larabee grunted with pleasure as he saw its roots drag up great gouts of dirt, making his task with the next trees that much easier.

Daylight had come before he had the cut choked with a tangle of fallen timber. They might, he thought dryly, just try to hack their way through it. But if he had judged Reardon right, the man was in too great a hurry. He would be more likely to risk the other trail, even though he might know of its dangers.

Now Larabee worked his way back to the other trail, again leaving clear sign. He swung around the first deadfall he made, going left toward the base of the mountains. The snow on the ground deepened as he climbed. And finally he was behind a long ridge that had kept the scouring wind away so that the tall spires and runs of rock, the ground itself, were deep with crusted snow.

Finding a protected spot, he made camp. He guessed that he would have time for a few hours' sleep before the mule train reached the junction. After that he could only hope they would take the bait and follow his tracks.

He grunted. And then—then he had to find a way to lead them into the middle of the trap itself. And a way to do it without getting shot down first.

CHAPTER SEVENTEEN

Kessler stared down at the clear tracks going down the wider of the two trails. 'I say the woman tricked us, Reardon. Those are Larabee's tracks.'

'He went over the cliff!' Lynn cried. 'I saw him.'

Kessler said flatly, 'I trailed Larabee and that chestnut long enough to know its hoofprints when I see 'em.'

Reardon spoke softly: 'Either Larabee tricked you, my dear, or you've both been tricking us. I hope for your sake it's the first.' He nodded to Kessler. 'If those are Larabee's tracks, that means he's got a good start on us. He's probably trying to reach an Army post to give them warning that we're coming.'

'He ain't too far ahead,' Kessler said. 'The sign is too fresh. I say me and Briggs ride on ahead and try to catch him.'

'There's no real need for hurrying down that trail,' Reardon said. He chuckled. 'According to the old-timer who mapped this country for me, you'd have to have wings to cross all the canyons that have bridges gone, and you'd have to have the luck of the devil to pick the right canyon of five that lie not too far ahead. My guess is that Larabee will be forced to find a way over to this other trail. It's the passable one.'

'It don't look it!'

'It didn't to Larabee either,' Reardon pointed out. He chuckled again. 'The big joke on him is that if he does cross over and takes this narrower trail—and if he manages to stay ahead of us—he won't come out near any Army post. He'll come out very close to our cache.'

'By God,' Kessler said, 'And if he does that, we'll have him pinned. Because once he gets back in them lava hills, there ain't but one way out: down the trail we'll be going up!'

Reardon nodded. 'My thinking exactly. But we can't take any chances. Send two of your men down the trail Larabee took. The rest of us and the mules will go the other route. A mile or so along, there's a place to cross over from one to the other. We can find out then just how far he went.'

Kessler gave the orders and Briggs, along with a squat miner named Farley, rode down the wide trail. Then Kessler started the mule string down the narrower trail.

'Easy going here,' he said. 'A ways along, there won't hardly be any snow.'

Reardon looked up at the sky. 'I don't like that scud of clouds,' he said. 'We could get some more.'

Lynn rode in silence either alongside or just ahead of Reardon. He hadn't tied her hands, but short of that she was obviously a prisoner.

Thinking of what Larabee had told her some days ago, she wondered why he had taken the obvious trail. The only conclusion she could come to was that he planned some sort of trick to get her free. He obviously wasn't running away, leaving her behind, or he wouldn't have been so careless with his tracks.

The thought buoyed her until the men ahead stopped suddenly and she heard Kessler's voice lifted in a curse. 'Blocked!'

Reardon rode forward, leaving Lynn. She followed and stared at the tangle of trees filling the cut between the two high walls of rock. Even to her unpracticed eye, the lay of this country was clear enough. Except for going directly south toward the other trail, there was no way to move. This trail was effectively blocked until someone put in a hard two days' work clearing out the deadfall.

A shout came from the south and Briggs rode into sight. 'Larabee's tracks come this way . . .' He broke off as he stared at the blocked trail. 'Some others went back south too. He musta made them when he saw this,' he suggested.

'You ain't making sense,' Kessler snarled at him. 'Which way did his tracks go last?'

Briggs climbed to the ground and drew a rough map with a stick. 'Down that other trail a ways, there's some fresh-fallen trees. Then there's tracks coming here. About halfway, there's tracks going back from here but they don't go all the way back to the downed trees. They angle off southwest. And a piece down the trail, there's a place where a man and two horses made camp not more'n a day ago.'

Reardon scowled. 'Briggs, you keep an eye on Miss Graham. Kessler, let's go take a look. Larabee's up to something.'

They were gone a good hour and when they returned, Lynn saw that they were arguing. 'As I see it,' Kessler said, 'Larabee went partway down that wide trail—to mislead us—and then cut over to this one. He figured we'd have to backtrack with the mules and that'd give him an extra half day's jump on us. Then he sees the deadfall, so he goes back to the other trail. But he don't want us getting too close too fast, so he tries to block it by cutting them trees across it.'

'And I say Larabee's cleverer than that,' Reardon answered. 'He's trying to trick us into something, but I don't know what.'

'It don't matter much,' Kessler growled. 'We got to chance the other trail for a ways at least. Then maybe we can find a way back to this one.'

Reardon had his map out and was studying it. 'There's a way. You can follow a ridge right after you come out of the five canyons.' He swore softly. 'The trouble is that the man who gave me this map was using a copy given to him. He'd never been here. And on his copy it didn't show which of the five canyons is the right one.'

'We got no choice,' Kessler argued. He squinted at the sky, thicker with clouds now. 'I say get moving until we come to them canyons. Sooner or later we'll find the right one. We got men enough to chouse down all of them. Now let's ride or Larabee'll have a start we never can make up.'

Reardon looked at the forest through which he and Kessler had just ridden. 'I think we can pick up some time on Larabee by running the mules straight across. We've packed down a pretty fair trail by now.'

Kessler waited no longer but ordered the men to put the mules in motion. He started out ahead, Briggs riding close to him. Reardon signaled to Lynn. 'Come on, my dear. And again I hope that for your sake this isn't a trick of Larabee's—and yours.'

'Brooks, how many times do I have to tell you . . .'

Smiling, he rode wordlessly on. She followed, feeling true fear for the first time now. In the short time she had been with Reardon in these mountains, she had come to realize just how ruthless he was, how driven by his need for the money the guns and ammunition represented. That he might be helping to slaughter innocent people, Indians and settlers alike, seemed to have no meaning for him.

When they reached the wider trail, Farley

was waiting. He said, 'I rode up a ways and had a look see. I picked up Larabee's tracks again. But he didn't stay on the trail long. He took off like he was going to climb them mountains there.'

Reardon said in quick decision, 'Farley, you stay here and when the mules come, work them around this deadfall Larabee laid across the trail. Then have the men take them up as far as Larabee's tracks go and stop there. We'll ride ahead and look the country over.'

He turned to Lynn. 'And you'll come along, my dear. If Mr. Larabee—or should I say Major—is waiting for us with a gun, you may be very useful.'

She gave him a withering look and rode in silence. The trail was barren for some distance except for Farley's sign. Then the tracks of Larabee's two horses came in from the timber on their right, went no more than a hundred yards up the trail and abruptly angled southerly toward the mountains.

'Why'n hell would he do that?' Kessler demanded. 'The snow's a lot thicker that way.'

'I'd say he's either laying a trap for us or trying to gain time some way,' Reardon said. 'Those look like fresh hoofprints to me.'

'Made today,' Kessler confirmed. 'He can't be too far ahead.' Not waiting for Reardon, he pushed up Larabee's tracks toward the mountains. Briggs followed, carrying his carbine across his lap now. Reardon hesitated,

176

shrugged, and motioned for Lynn to go on. He came last, herding her ahead of him.

* * *

Larabee lay on a ledge with a bank of snow protecting him from the rising wind. The first lazy flakes were beginning to fall but he could still see clearly enough. He smiled grimly as he watched the four figures coming doggedly along the trail he had made. Well back, he could see the dark, snaking line of the mule train. It had stopped for some time until Briggs had ridden back far enough to signal for it to come along.

Now, Larabee thought, they were committed. He had managed to funnel them into a long, narrow gulch. Soon they would come to the big snowslide he had triggered earlier, and then they could only stop and hunt for a place to camp. Even if this snow covered his last set of tracks—the ones he had half-heartedly brushed out as if trying to hide them—even then, they would find their way into the big cut that dug its way into the wall of mountain to their left. Short of turning and going back, they had no other choice.

He smiled again. And once in the cut, he would have them in the middle of the trap. He continued to watch as the four riders came close enough for him to see that Lynn was directly ahead of Reardon, and that the three men rode with their guns across their laps. Kessler was well ahead at this point, and he disappeared around a bend in the gulch. In a few moments he rode back into sight, holding up a hand.

'Big snowslide ahead. We can't get through. And there's no sign of Larabee's tracks up that way, anyway.' He pointed to the foot of the high ledge where Larabee lay watching. 'He took his horses that far and then nothing. I figure he's ducked in out of this storm and hid his tracks.'

'What he's hidden, we can find,' Reardon snapped. He was tired, obviously irritable and cold. 'We can't go on tonight anyway. I suggest you try to see just where Larabee did go.'

Kessler signaled to Briggs. When they were together, they rode to the base of the ledge and left their horses. They began slogging through the snow on foot, stopping every now and then to brush away snow and peer down.

'I found 'em!' Kessler shouted. 'They go around this rock!' He suddenly seemed to realize that Larabee might be close and he lifted his gun, staring around in the gathering dusk. Then he and Briggs backed to their horses, mounted, and rode forward.

Larabee remained where he was, enjoying this. Kessler and Briggs moved with caution, but they moved steadily. There was no cowardice here, he thought. They were risking their lives and they knew it.

178

Kessler stopped as Larabee's tracks became clearer, leading directly into a wide-mouthed opening between the ledge on which he lay and one directly east of it. 'Reardon, bring the girl and come along. I think we got him holed up!'

When Lynn and Reardon reached Kessler and Briggs, Kessler pointed through the opening. 'You can see all the way to the mountain wall if you squint hard enough,' he said. 'It looks like a dead end canyon. And Larabee's tracks go right in.'

'Where Larabee goes, we go,' Reardon said. He chuckled, lifted his gun, and aimed it at Lynn's back. 'Ride ahead, my dear. Just follow the sign.'

They went single file now, with Lynn in the lead. Once through the opening, Reardon halted her. He looked around, nodding. 'An interesting place. See those old mine shafts on the slope to the right, Kessler? They'll make fine shelter for the animals. And look straight through that narrow gut dead ahead, where Larabee's tracks go. There's a cave hollowed out of the mountain. A perfect place for us to camp out of the weather. Briggs, go back and hurry the mule train up this way. I want them settled in before it gets too dark.'

Briggs rode off. Kessler spat and said, 'A perfect place—if Larabee ain't waiting with a gun.'

Reardon prodded Lynn forward, almost to

the mouth of a cut so narrow that a horse and rider could barely make it through without scraping. The walls soared toward the snow-filled sky, running straight for some thirty feet and then curving away to form the sides of a bowl whose back end was the cave Reardon had seen. The distant tops of the sides of the cut were mounded with snow piled high. No wind got into this protected place, and the snow that had fallen these past days lay like cake topping, layer on layer, on the flat rocky tops of the sides of the cut.

Reardon said, 'Stop right there, my dear.' He lifted his voice. 'Larabee, come out empty-handed.'

Silence answered him. Kessler said, 'Maybe he ain't there. Maybe he found a way out.'

'We'll just ride in and see,' Reardon answered. He shouted again. 'One shot, Larabee, one trick—and Miss Graham will be dead!'

Lynn led the way through the cut. Now they were out of Larabee's sight. He could only lie on the ledge and wait. Shortly Reardon and Lynn returned, Kessler following.

'He didn't get out of that,' Reardon said. 'Not unless he climbed three hundred feet of sheer mountain face. No, he's here somewhere, watching us.' He turned his head. 'Kessler, take a look toward that slope where the mine shafts are. See if he put his horses up there and then covered his tracks.'

'And if he's in one of them tunnels, I get shot!'

'Only if he doesn't care whether or not Miss Graham dies,' Reardon said loudly. He laughed suddenly. 'In fact, if Larabee doesn't show himself in thirty seconds, I'm going to shoot her. In the leg first. Larabee knows what a carbine can do to flesh and bone at this range.'

He paused and looked around. 'Don't you, Larabee?'

Larabee lay on the ledge. He was no longer smiling. His trick had worked, all right; he had trapped them. Only it had worked too well. Because in trapping them, he'd trapped himself as well.

Taking a deep breath, he called, 'Hold your fire, Reardon. I'm coming down there— unarmed.'

CHAPTER EIGHTEEN

Reardon sipped his coffee and stretched his legs towards the crackling fire. 'Have you figured out why I haven't killed you, Larabee?'

Larabee, sitting near Lynn, said quietly, 'You think I know which canyon will get us out of here and up on that ridge that leads to the other trail.'

'I know that you know,' Reardon corrected him. 'Otherwise, you wouldn't have let yourself be boxed in. You made the snowslide that blocked the gulch, didn't you?' At Larabee's faint smile, he went on, 'And I suspect that somehow you made that deadfall in the cut on the other trail. You led us in here—to trap us.'

He looked around. 'I can't see how. But it makes no difference now. As soon as daylight comes, you're going to lead us through the right canyon.'

'I don't seem to have much choice,' Larabee said. Finishing his coffee, he stood up. 'I'm tired. I'm going to sleep.'

Lynn rose too and he walked with her to where her tent was pitched against the rear wall of the shallow cave. For the first time since Larabee had surrendered, she spoke. 'I'm sorry, Clint. I've made a complete mess of this. Brooks never did believe my story.'

'You had no choice but to try.'

'If I hadn't come . . . hunting you . . . this never would have happened.'

He said softly, 'Get some sleep and be ready to move fast if I wake you before daylight.' Turning, he went to where his blankets lay. Pulling off his boots, he readied himself for sleep. It came at once, quick and violent.

*   *   *

Larabee awoke as quickly as he had fallen asleep. He lay quietly assessing the situation. His head was turned toward the opening of the shallow cave and he could see the snow against the light of the low fire burning. The flakes were coming down thickly now, fat and heavy as they had been during that first storm. Larabee could see that a full six inches had come down since the snow began in early afternoon.

Larabee was grateful for the snow. It meant that much longer a time of safety for Lynn and himself. He knew without any doubt that, once he had led Reardon through the canyon and onto the ridge that ran over to the other trail, both of them would be shot. Reardon could afford to do nothing else. So the longer the weather continued bad, the longer it would take Larabee to get Reardon to where he wanted to go.

Larabee closed his eyes and slept again, seeking a few more hours or so of rest before daylight. He awoke this time to bright moonlight shining on freshly fallen snow and to the stirring of a wet, warm wind on his face. He swore under his breath. A chinook was coming. Out there in the open it would be rolling out of the southwest, its warmth cutting at the snow like a forge-heated knife. And then it would bring the rains to wash away the last remnants of Larabee's hopes of using the snow as a weapon against Reardon and his men.

Those extra days, even extra hours, that he had counted on to delay Reardon and to find a workable plan of escape—they were being blown away on that rising, warm wind.

Larabee lay a few moments longer, turning over in his mind the vague plan he had concocted during his long wait for the arrival of the mule train. But at the time it had seemed so unnecessary—and so unlikely of success if he did have to use it—that he had tossed it aside. Now he brought it back and examined it a second time.

The chances of success looked no better than they had before, but work as it might, his mind could find no better solution. Grunting softly, Larabee sat up slowly and looked around. The blanketed mounds scattered about between Lynn's tent and the fire were motionless. Larabee counted seven sleepers. That meant there were two up and about. One he could see across the side of the fire, sitting with his back propped against the rock wall of the cave. The other . . . ?

Larabee risked standing. There was no sign of the other man. Boldly, Larabee pulled on his boots and crossed to the fire. Despite the warm wind, the air still held a deep chill that bit through his shirt. He flapped his arms about himself.

The guard looked up and lifted his carbine. Larabee squatted and reached for a mug and the coffeepot. 'Can't sleep,' he mumbled.

'Get back to your blankets.'

'Don't be a damn fool,' Larabee said. 'Do you think I'm going to bolt for it in my shirtsleeves? Run out and make myself a target in the moonlight? I came for some coffee.'

The man grinned through bearded lips. 'Yeah, I guess you ain't going far, come to think of it. Besides, if you got past me, where'd you be?'

Larabee let some coffee dregs dribble into the mug. 'Dodging the bullets of the man watching the stock,' he said. It was a guess, but a good one, he saw, as the man nodded.

Larabee set down the coffeepot and emptied the dregs into the fire. 'Is this all you've got?'

'More over here,' the man said. He leaned back again but his rifle remained at the ready.

Larabee moved around the fire and lifted the pot the man indicated. He poured a cup two-thirds full. 'Want some?'

'I'm running over with it.'

Larabee set the pot down, lifted the cup to his lips and blew softly. As he straightened up, he made two swift, blended moves. His wrist snapped, sending a stream of scalding liquid into the guard's face. At the same time, he jumped forward, his hand chopping down to silence the man just as a scream burbled into his throat. Larabee caught his gun and laid it aside. Quickly now, he dragged the man to one side, out of the firelight and away from the sleeping men. He bound and gagged the guard with his own belt and kerchief and then returned for the gun.

The sleepy voice of Kessler said, 'What's the racket, Poston?'

Larabee tried to imitate the guard's surly voice. 'I thought I heard a cat. But it wasn't nothing.'

Kessler's grunt was followed by a snore. Larabee waited a long moment and then slid along the wall to the rear of the cave. He crossed to Lynn's tent, knelt and reached in, clamping a hand over her mouth. She came upright, fingers clawing at his arm.

He whispered, calming her. He took away his hand as he felt her head bob in answer to his swift instructions. Then he moved on, back to his blankets. He worked into his greatcoat. A glance at the sleeping men showed no change. Taking a deep breath, he padded over to the heap of supplies. He was feeling through them, hoping to find his or Lynn's weapons when she drifted alongside him.

'I saw Brooks put them in his saddlebags,' she whispered.

Larabee nodded and motioned to her. Together they eased out of the cave and slid through the soft wet layer of snow that edged the sheer cliffs rimming this bowl. It was slow, chilling work, but they finally reached the narrow gut where the wall of the bowl folded into its side.

Larabee glanced toward the cave. There was no sign of activity there. He led the way to the far end of the gut and stopped at the beginning of the wider space. Now they could hear the sounds of restless horses and mules coming from the mine tunnels. On the ledge that fronted the tunnels, a small fire threw the shadow of a standing man in sharp relief. Larabee spoke softly to Lynn, outlining his plan.

'Can you do it?' he asked her. 'If he spots you, you haven't got much chance without a gun.'

'I can do it,' she said. 'You're the one who's taking the risk.'

He touched her shoulder and then watched as she slid through shadow, gliding toward the far end of the ledge. He waited patiently until he saw her at the very edge of the reach of the flickering fire. Now he moved, going boldly into the open and toward the ledge.

The guard moved forward, his rifle lifted. Larabee again tried to imitate Poston's voice. 'You see a big cat come this way?' Then he lifted a hand. 'Over to the left side of the ridge?'

A head swiveled and then turned back. 'I don't see nothing.'

Lynn had disappeared. Larabee waited, wondering how long it would be until the guard realized he couldn't be Poston. The man took another step forward, now thrusting his head in Larabee's direction. 'You . . .' A dark form moved up behind him. An arm lifted and fell. He crumpled forward, his rifle falling into the snow.

Blowing out his breath, Larabee raced up to the ledge. Lynn stood with a handgun held by the barrel. She was trembling. He touched her hand. 'Good work.'

Handing her the carbine, he dragged the guard back into a tunnel and tied and gagged him as he had Poston. Now they both moved quickly, working together as if they had done this time and again. They saddled their horses and loaded their pack animals from the bulk of supplies that that had been left in an unused tunnel. Larabee found his own guns in Reardon's saddlebags, and now he felt better.

'Take a look, but keep out of sight,' he told her.

Lynn rode her sorrel down from the ledge

and into a position where she could see through the narrow gut to the cave. She returned to find Larabee prying open a box of ammunition.

'No movement yet,' she said briefly. 'Are you ready?'

He opened the box and pulled out a keg of what was still called musket powder, the kind of powder used for the heavier field pieces. Another box yielded percussion caps for the older types of weapons, and a third gave him some empty, large shell casings. These he carried within range of the firelight.

'Can you go back and keep an eye on the cave? I'll need ten minutes.'

She nodded and rode away again. He crouched, carefully fixing the shell casings by borrowing an old trick from the Sioux Indians. Punching a hole in the head of each shell, he crammed in percussion caps and then dropped in a .44 bullet to provide a hitting surface for the cap. That done, he filled the shells carefully with powder and closed off the ends. When he finished, he had eight heavy, dangerously touchy charges of powder.

He mounted the chestnut and, carrying the shells gingerly suspended against various soft parts of his body, rode down to where Lynn watched.

'All quiet,' she said. 'But the moon is sinking. They'll be up and stirring soon.'

'Sooner than they expected to, I hope,' he

said with a tight smile. 'Just keep a close watch. If they do spot you, don't start shooting. Pull back so they can't get an angle on you.'

She nodded. Larabee left the saddle and laid the shells carefully in the snow. Taking two, he thrust them against the base of the front of the narrow gut, one against the rock on each side. Now he took three of the remaining six shells and fixed them to his clothing so that they would be protected from hitting anything hard. Taking a deep breath, he started climbing the high side of the gut that was nearest the ledge and the low fire.

It was a slow, torturous trip, requiring Larabee to work back and forth up the steeply sloping rock, fitting a toe in solidly before he moved his other foot, making sure of each handhold. Finally he dragged himself to the top and burrowed into the great mound of snow stretching there. Resting a moment, he eased his three shells free and began placing them. He scooped a hollow at the base of the hard-packed snow and worked in a shell so that the end with the percussion cap faced outward and projected a few inches into the open. He did this three times, spacing the shells evenly along the length of the ledge.

He went back down more quickly, dropping the last dozen feet into a snowbank. He glanced at Lynn. She nodded, indicating that all remained quiet.

Now he had to work his way up the left-hand rock face and repeat the process. With the moon gone behind a distant mountain and no firelight, this was slower and more agonizing. But finally he was back on the ground, trembling a little and feeling the chill against his sweat-soaked body.

Lynn signaled to him. He mounted the chestnut and hurried toward her. 'They're stirring,' she said. 'How long can we wait?'

'We have to wait for enough light to see our targets,' he said. 'I'll watch here. You get the pack animals over to the entrance. If we can't do anything else, we can ride and hope to stay ahead of them.'

'Ahead of nine men when we'll be breaking trail and they'll be using our work to make better time?'

Larabee nodded, but didn't put his hopelessness into words. She was right, of course. Their one chance was for light enough to see their targets before any of the seven men discovered they were missing and started for them. They might be able to shoot one or two charging through the gut, but to do so would mean putting themselves into the position of being picked off by someone behind.

Larabee studied the camp as Lynn rode away. He saw Kessler rise, stretch, and look around. Then he heard the man's deep bellow, 'Larabee's gone! So's the woman!'

Larabee rode to the very edge of the gut.

'Freeze, all of you!' he shouted. 'Don't reach for anything—and that includes your boots.'

Kessler made a darting movement toward the guns lying by his blankets. Larabee snapped a shot from his carbine. It whistled by Kessler's ear and struck against the rear wall of the cave.

'Next time I put it in you,' Larabee warned.

Reardon was standing now. 'Just what do you think you've gained?' he demanded.

Without looking upward, Larabee could sense the first daylight coming to wipe the darkness from the sky. 'Considerable,' he answered.

Lynn rode alongside him, her gun ready. Reardon laughed. 'Very clever, Larabee. You not only get out of the trap but take the bait with you. All right, go ahead and ride. Or do you think you can gun all of us down from there?'

Larabee said carefully, backing the chestnut slowly as he talked. 'You have supplies enough in there to last you a week if you eat easy. By that time, the Army should be along to get you out.'

He lifted a hand and signaled to Lynn. She swung her sorrel to the right. Larabee sent the chestnut to the left. He could no longer see into the gut but he could hear the shouts, the snapped commands of Kessler and Reardon.

'Can you see the targets?' he shouted to Lynn.

'Barely.'

'Then start shooting!'

Lifting his carbine, he took aim on the end of the shell that thrust out of the snow near the inner end of the gut. He squeezed the trigger —and missed. Swearing softly, he fired again. His shot caught the shell squarely, driving the percussion cap against the .44 bullet inside. The powder exploded, sending a great gout of snow lifting upward to slide into the gut. It pulled more snow with it. At the same time Lynn scored from the other side and more snow cascaded down.

Kessler cried, 'He's going to block us in here!'

Larabee moved to his right and took aim on the second shell. He could barely see it in the dim light and he needed three shots before it exploded. Across from him, out of sight, Lynn was still firing at her target. When she hit it, Larabee hit his third shell at almost the same instant. The combined force of the two blasts sent almost all of the remaining mounds of snow sliding down from the ledge to choke the gut. Larabee looked for Lynn's third shell but it had gone with the snow. Suddenly he heard it explode, sending a great gout of white powder up. It settled back slowly on the now strangely still air.

'One more chore,' Larabee said, riding to the front of the snow-filled gut, 'and then we can get underway. If they can dig out, they won't get far before the Army has the trails all blocked off.'

Now he sought for the two shells he had placed at the bottom of the front edges of the gut. Loose snow had buried them and so he climbed down from the chestnut and began digging carefully with his hands. Full daylight had come before he located both and had their ends exposed.

Mounting again, he and Lynn rode to the far entrance. Larabee lifted his rifle and sighted on one of the shell casing ends. Lynn took aim on the other.

They fired. Both bullets struck squarely. The powder exploded, ripping now at rock instead of packed snow. There was a moment of thick silence, shaken only by the echo of the explosions. Then the two front edges of the gut slowly, achingly caved inward. They crashed down in a great heap of rubble, filling the already snow-choked end of the gut.

'I'll give them a week at the least to fight their way out,' Larabee said. He tied his bay to the rear of the chestnut. 'Shall we ride?'

'Yes, Major.'

Larabee smiled at her and led the way into the open—and back into an angling warm wind that seemed to slice the snow from under their horses' hooves as they rode.

*   *   *

They sat at the junction of the narrow trail with the wide wagonroad that ran up this eastern backbone of Idaho Territory. Larabee looked at the muddy stretch ahead of them.

'I think I'd rather have snow,' he said, hunching against the rain the chinook had brought. 'But it isn't over a day's ride to the Army post.'

He led the way onto the main road and started north. Lynn had room now to ride alongside. She said, 'What will you do when this is over, Clint?'

'A lot depends on what news I hear of the Indians,' he said. 'How touchy they've got these last weeks.' He shrugged the problem aside for the moment. 'But right now and for some time I'll be busy. With the information you got listening to Reardon and Kessler, we should be able to locate the cache back in those lava rocks. But it will still take time. Then I've got to make out an armload of reports.'

He grinned across at her. 'Come to think of it, you'll be making depositions until you're sick of them.'

'If they hang Brooks, I'll be glad to,' she said thinly.

'Do you still regret not having killed him?'

'No,' she said. 'I want no blood on my conscience. When I struck down that guard, I knew that I couldn't bring myself to kill.'

They rode on silently. The mud slowed

them and finally they were forced to stop and make camp with the Army post a good morning's day's ride still ahead. As they sat finishing their meal, Lynn said, 'After everything is taken care of, what then, Clint? You never did answer my question.'

'After the Indian wars that are bound to come,' he said softly, with quiet sadness, 'then maybe I'll turn in my resignation.'

She looked at him in surprise. 'And do what?'

'The same thing I did as a boy and as I did for a time when I first left the Army. Go into ranching.'

She seemed to be laughing at him. 'Then your looking around Glory Hole for a ranch wasn't all in the line of duty?'

'It was at the time,' Larabee said. 'But the more I think of that country, the more I find myself liking it.'

She poured him some coffee. 'You wouldn't be interested in buying a half interest in a going hotel, would you?'

Larabee looked up, caught her smile, and answered it. 'No,' he said. 'But I just might be interested in a half interest in a good ranch. Say one like the Lazy B.'

'I'll make you a good price,' she said, 'if you want to take an option now.'

'Always the businesswoman.' He laughed.

She was suddenly serious. 'Not always,' she said. 'Someday the hurt for Dan will go away.

Then I'll be just a woman, waiting for a man as good as he was.'

Larabee reached out and touched her hand with his fingertips. Her skin was cold and she was trembling slightly.

He said, 'I don't think you'll have to wait too long. I don't know if you see me as good as Dan Peters, but I'd like to think you'd wait until I could come to Glory Hole so you could find out.'

She said softly as she turned away, 'I've already decided that.' She walked off into the darkness. Larabee sat and watched her go, knowing that she wouldn't be far away, knowing that in some ways she would never be far from him again.